# CONTENTS

# FRICTIONS

An Anthology of Fiction by Women

EDITED BY ANNA GIBBS AND ALISON TILSON

SYBYLLA COOPERATIVE PRESS AND PUBLICATIONS LTD
MELBOURNE. AUSTRALIA.

Published by Sybylla Co-operative Press and Publications Ltd, 193 Smith St,
Fitzroy, Vic. 3065

National Library of Australia card number and
ISBN 0 908 205 02 3

Cover design by Anne Lorraine.
Typeset by Correct Line Graphics, 193 Smith St, Fitzroy, Vic. 3065 and by
Barthes Productions, North Fitzroy, 3068.
Printed by Sybylla Co-operative Press and Publications Ltd.
First edition published with the assistance of the Literature Board, Australia
Council.

Thanks to all those who have assisted this project financially and in the
process of production.

# INTRODUCTION

*"What about feminism. Do you see yourself as a feminist
writer? Part of the new wave?
No. I am going through a phase of refusing to talk about
feminism as a separate topic. I believe it is integral,
fundamental, ex- and im-plicit, inseparable from everything. I don't think, by the way, that we actually know
what a feminist writer is. Is it someone who is meticulous
in her use of pronouns and reclaimed (redefined) words,
fastidious in the casting of characters? Is it someone who,
being a woman and a good (bad) writer, uncovers some
truth about the world? Is it someone, blissfully unaware,
whom feminists claim, for her purity, perhaps? Is it
the woman who, being of sound mind and with a nose
for business, puts money into publishing and sees her
name irrefutably on the title page? Is it a Bronte or a
Parker and should feminist writers all be able to sit in
a room together drinking tea and never being tense?"*

Jan McKemmish
from *A Notebook: Non-narrative Fiction and Intervention*

If it's difficult to define what makes a 'feminist writer', in the course
of editing this book we've found it equally difficult to define 'feminist
writing'. When we advertised for copy, we specified only that the
writing be by women, thinking it possible that some writers mightn't
consider their work feminist if it wasn't realist narrative and didn't
take 'women's lives' as its subject. That famous formula 'by women,

about women, for women' lets feminist editors down in the end, we realised. It could just as easily apply to much of the writing that comes out in *Cleo* or *Cosmopolitan* as to books that come out from feminist presses. And it leaves aside the possibility of a feminist perspective on *any* situation, threatening to confine feminist fiction to the kitchen of so-called 'women's issues'. The difficulty of definition raises questions about the usefulness of the term 'feminist writing'.

In fact, defining a category of writing that could be neatly packaged and labelled 'feminist' may not be a useful strategy at all, if it allows people to forget that *all* writing is political – including the kind that wishes to appear neutral. Moreover, even when writing specifically presents itself as feminist, its effects can't be precisely calculated, since writing 'dates', contexts change, readers disagree about what's feminist and what's not. Feminism isn't homogeneous. In short, to try to categorize writing as 'feminist' or not is to overlook the effects of reading. Reading, after all, is just as much subject to social and political constraints as writing. This is the case not only because individual readers bring to the work as much diversity in terms of sex, class, etc., as individual writers, but because 'making sense' of something is a social (and therefore political) procedure. One way to make sense of a text is to give it a literary context. Mary Shelley's *Frankenstein* read as science fiction produces a very different interpretation from a reading in the light of, for example, the tradition one feminist critic terms "female gothic". It makes better sense, therefore, to talk of feminist textual production than feminist writing. 'Textual production' is an effect of both writing *and* reading, and the term also emphasises the material conditions under which writing is circulated. Publishing houses and distribution networks determine not only which writing circulates publicly, but how it does so. The cover of a book tells people which section of the bookshop or library it fits in, whether it's fiction or non-fiction, belongs to 'high' or 'popular' culture – tells people, in short, how to read it. For us, to publish with a feminist press is to indicate the kind of intervention we wish to make into various social, political and literary economies.

Not all the writing in this book presents itself overtly as feminist. But a feminist perspective is nevertheless the *raison d'etre* of the collection itself: women are still under-represented in most mainstream anthologies. And it was crucial to our *selection* of writing, to our reading of the several hundred manuscripts sent to us, and our perception of their relationship to each other. Choosing material was not easy. It involved not so much weighing which writing had the strongest effect, as counterposing different kinds of effect. Much of the writing we chose is conscious of the act of writing itself, of writing as an activitiy that constructs a relationship with a (fictional) reader. Many pieces refuse to engage in traditional story telling and instead take up and play with readers' expectations of or about narrative, forcing them actively to examine the way they make sense of what they read, as well as *what* sense they make of it. We didn't want to dismiss narrative, but rather to place it in a perspective that gives credence to other kinds of writing as well, some of which is not readily accepted by mainstream publishers. Since we are both also writers, we were often influenced by what found echoes in our own work. Sometimes we were fascinated by the foreign.

Rather than seeking to impose a prescription for a fictional feminist orthodoxy, we wanted to allow different kinds of writing and different points of view to comment on each other. Which is why the pieces we have chosen don't necessarily sit easily in the same book, regardless of whether their authors could sit in a room drinking tea and never being tense. Often there is tension even within the writing of a single author. The danger of an anthology is that it homogenises what it contains between its covers, but we would like to think that the frictions in ours speak as loudly as the fictions.

We cannot say with certainty what sparks these f(r)ictions will generate, nor where they will land. But we hope there will be fire. We are attempting, with this anthology, not so much to say something more, as to say something different. We go along with the spirit of Gertrude Stein's assertion that "It is not clarity that is desirable but force". Her own work, she maintained, was as clear as mud, but, she said, "mud settles, and clear streams run on".

To change metaphors again: we wish to do more than help redress a balance: we want to upset the economy.

**Anna Gibbs**

**Alison Tilson**

# SNEJA GUNEW

## Reading

In my sleep I try to retain my grasp of German and through that talisman to reach my father's language, of which I was once taught the alphabet — not by my father, by a substitute. I was told to master the language of this third place.

So, in my swashbuckling dreams I tried gender-hopping to master my destiny. As I learnt the daylight language I was conscious of the shadows of the other code, the anachronistic forbidden language of the master-race, mediated by childhood fairytales and by my mother transformed.

It was that language, in baroque gothic curlicues, which first opened its doors to me — signs into stories. The process stays but that language now transmutes only my dreams into gold. It has staked its claim on my inner world. The Jesuits exaggerated; at four it was already too late.

From the shadows, my mistress master language sabotages my daylight steps to clay. I am so slow. At night, with my mermaid's tail I refuse all offers from land. It is the only time I can swim.

## Inquiry into Race

Where do I come from, what am I, now?

It used to be enough to say — "My mother is German; my father Bulgarian." People usually latched onto the more familiar first part, in spite of the fact that my personal cliché arose in response to their own cliché queries concerning my name. My name is Bulgarian and therefore requires support in this vacuum.

It's not so easy now. My source of reference, the arbiter for things Bulgarian, is silent now. And my usual method of referring to the written word is blocked — I cannot read my father's language. The few translations in existence, in English, are not to be trusted and, being open to all, cut across my satisfaction in having access to the occult.

Confronted with those closed, swarthy faces at the funeral, I recalled the Bulgarian picnics of my childhood. They are not much help. We did not attend many. They were too unrestrainedly ethnic, too woggish (from another point of view), not middle-class enough for my father, who believed he had made his choice of allegiance when he became a student in Germany and never saw his motherland, or his mother, again.

His own identity, therefore, is not secure. All his women seemed to be leggy blondes, until my mother. What Teutonic paradise was he seeking? His German was impeccable — both spoken and written. He returned from a visit some years ago with Bavarian costume-pieces — civilian.

In German, 'rassisch' has connotations of 'breeding', similar to the way in which the Anglo-Irish speak of a horse, or of a woman — best of all, a woman on horse-back, a thoroughbred centaur.

The Bulgarians at the funeral had shades of my yellow skin and round faces and flat Russian noses. Not my father and I. Our noses came from . . . probably Turkish (secretly I always hoped so) though my father denied it vehemently as slander. Like all Bulgarians he asserted that five hundred years of Ottoman rule had left no trace. Proudly, and paradoxically, he drew part of his self-image from his peasant grandparents, the ones in Varna, on the Black Sea, who worked the vineyard.

Varna and Melbourne on the headstone locate him accurately within the inaccuracy of the Macedonian section of the cemetery. There are not enough Bulgarians in Melbourne to support a separate church. Most of his friends, at one time, had German wives. Australia has always found Germans to be acceptable candidates for immigration. But did my father succeed in his redefinitions?

My great-aunt, the baronness, meeting me at the airport in Munich in '68, recognized me immediately because I looked foreign. She, indeed, dark herself, was *rassisch* and too proud to ever link herself with any alien blood. With the arrogance of the Pharaohs, she has lived with her sister for decades. She is, no doubt, racist.

## MO[T]HE[R] / H[T]OME[R]

In my mother's dreams are many mansions and none include the house she has occupied for 30 years. Neither the house nor her body expressed her. She was embarrassed by both and always covering up flaws. 'Primitiv' was a word we heard often and in her usage it signified retarded growth and not primordial energy. Her own body would have inspired primitive worship, a scaled down magna mater, but the house would at best have provoked arson.

Her feelings reached a crisis point after my father's death when she found herself in a panic to sell the house because clearly now it, and not the new one in the country which my father would never inhabit, would incorporate their marriage.

That corner mansion of makeshift extensions had been the basis of most of their quarrels — those not concerned with our own extensions into adulthood. It was always in a state of becoming and reflected my mother's being only through my father's doing, or promising to do. Woman is: man does . . . not. While paint flaked and boards sagged and each year new kittens were dropped through the hole in the roof by their protective mothers, my father could yet not bring himself to sub-contract even basic repairs. It represented too painful a comment on his own being. His camouflage was to discourse regularly on my mother's lack of household discipline. But in pursuit of her glamorous mirage, my mother could justify the tedium of housework only after extensive renovations.

Occasionally her purifying tornado would burst beyond the house over the garden and engender intricate blueprints. For months we would stumble through a network of muddy trenches — a freeze-frame Japanese floating world. After she erected a rockery snug against the walls, the house retaliated by spawning earwigs. My youngest brother, who took words literally at that stage, refused to go to bed unless his ears were wrapped up in a scarf. The plague receded after the rockery was removed and the scarf left no trace (so far as I can tell) on my brother's later personality.

Finally my parents compromised by agreeing to have their future domestic productions sited and built by others elsewhere. Even then my mother had to bow to economic necessity, to make do as she always had to make do in this country. But she did hold fast to one accessory — the notion of a dining-table large enough to seat the whole expanded family, as though this would ensure our dynastic preservation, our survival on alien soil.

She is still waiting for it and we are dwindling, as she feared.

# KATE LLEWELLYN

## The Balts

When we first went to the farm, people who came to Australia from Europe were called Balts. Whether they came from the Baltic States or not didn't matter to most people and not at all, as far as I know, to my Mother. My Father may have known where the Baltic States were, but my Mother wouldn't have been interested. She had a curious determination to refuse any information which wouldn't, in her opinion, be useful. How to cure nailbiting in a child, or croup or measles or whooping cough or which child to gather up first to take to the air raid shelter in the backyard if there was ever an air raid were all of immediate and rivetting interest to her. But she was impressed by signs of braininess in others — such as if they were a good bridge player or, as she said, well read. She always told us our Father was very well read, though I know now he wasn't. He did belong to Foyle's Book Club and had a black table with revolving book shelves underneath filled with his books. They were not about Baltic people, nor, for that matter, Australia. They were by English novelists and were about life in South Africa, India or an English village, and were by such people as Warwick Deeping and Rebecca West. I read them over and over and became very familiar with locust plagues in South Africa and the problems of novelists of the 30s and 40s waiting for publishers' advances and living on sheep's head stew. One author was married in his book to a woman called Tansy whose hair fell in a thick wing over one side of her face. Occasionally I still see someone with this hairstyle.

My Mother went alone to the farm with my three small brothers. My Father stayed behind to finish his work and I stayed to care for him. He liked Welsh rabbit made from stale cheese which we got at a reduced price from the grocer. I grated it into boiling milk and served it with raw chopped onions. My Mother didn't make these dishes as she said they made him smell. For two weeks we lived on Welsh rabbit and Irish stew.

We arrived at the farm after a drive of 240 miles in a small buckboard which had absolutely upright seats. It gave me a backache like the ones I was to become familiar with later when I began to menstruate. We found my Mother in a strained and nervous state. The first thing she said to me was: "Did you clean the bathroom?" I said I hadn't. She began to ask what would the new people think and to say over and over how important it was to clean a bathroom when you leave a house. Packing up the kitchen and cleaning two weeks of rabbit saucepans had seemed quite enough for me, but I was sorry I hadn't done the bathroom.

My Mother had been sleeping badly. She kept a pepper pot under the pillow to throw at any Balt who made his way into the house. She also kept an axe under the bed. She'd been woken by noises several times and had thrown the pepper pot up and given herself awful sneezing fits. She said the Balts had an alarming habit of walking in the door as you opened it after they'd knocked. This, someone told her later, was because they came from a cold climate and sensibly stepped inside to stop the heat leaving the house. Whatever the truth of this, it calmed her, since she loved practicality better than almost anything else.

The Balts were all large blonde men and women and one day one came not only to buy eggs, but to ask if several of his friends could rent some of the old stone sheds to live in. My Mother said they weren't fit to live in but he convinced her they were better than the hostel which was, after all, only corrugated iron while the sheds had ceilings and cement floors. Finally my Mother agreed.

Soon after they moved in, the women began to help her in the house. This was to make up the rent which was eight shillings a week. "Have you seen Olga's nappies?" she'd say, "They're whiter than a row of angels' wings. You can say what you like about Balts, they're wonderfully clean people." The women made our beds so smooth and taut my Mother said she could have ironed on them. She had never had such excellent helpers, "They even rinse the washing three or four times till it runs clear!" she said. Gradually, in ways such as this, my Mother became friendly.

To me they remained tall, mysterious, silent people.

When Olga was sweeping the drive one day I asked her what she thought about going to hospital to have her baby which was due quite soon. I can't remember what she said, but she gave me to understand in strong terms that she wasn't looking forward to it. I put this away in my mind with my Mother's comment when I'd asked her what it was like having a baby. "It's like being run over by a train!" She loved my Father more than us, which was unusual in those days apparently. I knew that as her friends laughed (fondly, but as if she was a bit childish) when she looked up from the sink and said: "Oh here he comes!"

The Balts had several babies and my Mother had her photograph taken holding the baby each time and put it in our family album with "The Balts' baby" written underneath. The baby was wearing our christening robe. I had a feeling she was keen on doing this partly because she felt that as long as she held other people's babies she wouldn't have any more herself.

One family gave my Mother a teardrop pearl set in gold on a chain necklace. They had brought it from their country. She wore it to all our weddings.

When she met me at the railway station the other day, she drew up in her big black batmobile (which was my Father's Pontiac before he died) skidding on the gravel and sending her bowling balls rolling along the back seat. She was wearing the necklace but the pearl had been replaced with a perfectly round one. I asked her what had happened and she said she'd lost the teardrop pearl and had it replaced.

Nothing stays the same I know, and now the necklace is spoiled. But when my Mother dies I'm going to give it back to that family.

# Gone

Where did it go? That's what I keep asking myself, though I know the answer. In a bin. I know it's a funny thing to say, but if only I'd had some pain, it would've helped. There was nothing. No pain, no memory, nothing to see, nothing to feel. I weep for my grief. Greeted with curses it multiplied its cells for a few weeks. The best I can say is it left with its Mother's tears. That's all it ever had; not much. I suppose in Calcutta at times, they don't even get that.

I keep thinking about a sheep. When my friend gave birth to her fifth still-born baby, her husband went out into the paddock and brought in a baby lamb. That sheep must have wandered for days. That's how I feel. Nothing to see, nothing to find. Just a hole in the air. Gone. Important to no-one but me, but gone.

Do you wonder why I didn't just have it and then give it away, if I couldn't keep it myself. Well, of course I thought about it. I think I could have done it − I'm quite tough really − but I couldn't believe it'd have a decent life.

I've been watching tennis on T.V. in this heatwave. It's too hot to do anything else. The sight of all those ads of people hoe-ing into margarine or buying posh cars and bragging about it really shook me. I mean those ads are made for people who the researchers know will believe in all that. I couldn't help thinking that the people who live like that would be just the type to get an adopted baby. They'd seem so stable and such good providers.

I know it's a queer thing to say, but I felt if it wasn't going to have art in its life, I couldn't go through with all I knew lay ahead. And then I thought of unemployment and that book *Puberty Blues* and that didn't help either. Yet I can't help grieving.

It's true its Father is good and rich and clever and could afford a child and give it a decent life, but why ruin someone's life to give another one a chance? His wife would have found out if I'd had it. It's ironic really: it was sacrificed, in part, to save something I don't believe in. Marriage needs endless sacrifices. They even say so at weddings.

I keep wondering where it is. Is it a smile? It came and went fast as laughter.

What if it was a genius? An egotistical thought, I know. More likely it'd have Downes' Syndrome. I know that. The world can't deal with either very well. Yet it tries. I can't deny what I see around me. I still have faith. Resistant as the faith of those few cells. There's something. I see it every day. There's grace which never really left us. An old woman gives a nod when standing at her gate. There's wisdom too. Someone leans and puts their head into their hands and has a darn good think. I love that. Others walk daily to their shed and work even in a heatwave, and out come paintings, jewellery, sculpture or stained glass windows. Thoughts like that keep me going.

Don't misunderstand me, I'd do it again tomorrow. But I'd stay awake; just have a local anaesthetic. Then I'd comprehend. I know this is the sort of thing people don't talk about, but I have to understand.

The waiting was the worst part. The faith of those cells drove me nuts. In the hospital every five minutes was half an hour. I'd look at the clock and be amazed it had hardly changed. Then they came and dressed me. As if for an execution. Even a cap to keep the hair from my neck. I lay on a barouche. They were late. Another half hour passed. I wheeled myself along by pulling on the bed ends after I'd got another patient to unlock the wheels. I got out into the corridor and could see the anaesthetist gowned and ready through the theatre window. The surgeon wasn't there. A nurse came out and said: "Who left you here?" and pushed me back into the ward. I was ready, bathed, dressed, eager. I would have kissed the surgeon's hands to give him grace and skill and haste.

At last they came and wheeled me in. The anaesthetist asked me how I felt. "Alert." I said and waited for the needle in the vein. I should've stayed alert. When they'd finished I didn't believe it was done. I asked when they'd begin. It was done. Nothing. Gone.

My daughter has just come in and read this story and I said: "Well, what do you think of that?" She said: "Well, if you ask me Mrs. Travers, if you don't look out The Right To Life will use it. The way you put it, it's going to be grist to their mill." I said: "Warner, you never cease to surprise me — a woman of your experience having such insights?" "Well," she said, "You can't live all your adult life with such people as you, Mrs Travers, without getting an experience of one kind or another, and it looks to me as if it's far from clear that you're glad you had a doctor to do the job. I was worried you would've done the deed yourself if you weren't living in such a civilised society." "Thank you Warner my dear, whatever did I do to deserve you? Let's have a cup of tea and toast our good fortune."

## I Am My Own Companion

I feel like going out and getting a dose of the clap. Maybe
I wouldn't like the results, but just getting it would be good. At times
like this, doing something stinking is the only thing that really helps.
I've tried it. I've never got the clap, I admit. I must have a guardian
angel. Once when my boyfriend — who's married — and that's what
this is all about, as he's just admitted he fucked his wife twice last
weekend. Honestly, what do mistresses think men do with their
wives? Well, I know it goes on, of course, but I don't want to know
*when*, though I ask him all the time, but I hate it when I get the news.
Twice! Once, I could have handled, but twice! I mean that's not duty
is it, though he says it is. The deceitful pig. Well, as I was saying,
once when he asked: "Are you sure you won't get a social disease,
as they call it, on one of your little escapades?" I said: "No, I only
fuck middle class men." Which was pretty silly: I know the middle
class are far from exempt, and, if the truth's known, they probably
put it about a whole lot more with their multiple fucks and wives and
mistresses. But what I was really thinking was they usually wash a lot
and I felt that would make it OK. It's nonsense I suppose, but I keep
thinking it might help.

It's not hard to do something really low, it's easy. The last time I
did, a friend rang up and asked me to a party. I said I wasn't in the
mood and was already in my nightie. He said it'd be a great party and
half my friends would be there and it was given by a hot shot lawyer
at the Hilton, and I thought why not? It'd take my mind off that
other bastard (who wasn't married) and his: "Consider my bed your
bed" and finding someone else in it after I'd spent twelve nights
straight there, wanted a night at home alone and then changed my
mind at midnight.

There are times when the only thing to do is to get really low. Roll
in the gutter in a manner of speaking. That's why I don't care who it
is, or how stupid they are and if they're rich, so much the better.
I don't need to feel sorry for them as that's no use at all for this game.
God knows though it's a struggle not to feel sorry at times. Let's
face it, when men feel amorous they do the most childish things. And
I don't mean sucking your breasts. They can get really pathetic. You'd
hardly believe it, but even on a one night stand I've actually had them
say they're in love. Letters from Djakarta a week later declaring how

much I mean to them. They can't help it, I know, but the moment that happens I put the letters that follow unopened in the bin in my bedroom. Boredom. It's pathetic really, but the number of middle aged men who are lonely is too awful to think about. I reckon after a man turns 45 he should have someone walking in front of him with a red flag as they used to do with the first cars, to show he is a danger and can't look after himself.

I don't want to risk them phoning or writing, so I don't let them know my surname if I can help it. Never to see or hear from them is best. I had to laugh once. One said he'd ring me and I said: "Don't, I'll ring you." And he said: "But you don't know my name."

Another thing I'm careful about is not letting the man who's made me feel like getting low ever know what I do, so there's no chance of him thinking I'm trying to get even or feeling I've punished him. My current boyfriend knows I do it. That's because it's hard to hide this over a long period of time but he never knows *when* I do it and it only happens when I'm really disgusted. I am my own companion at these times.

Well, back to the cure. That particular party had food sent up from Room Service and a lot of bottles of wine and prints all round the room. I really felt like taking one home. The bloke who gave the party wouldn't have missed it. But when I get the need to be low, stealing isn't part of it. I'm quite scrupulous in my own way.

When the party ended, two of my friends offered me a lift home. I said: "No thanks, I'm staying the night." They didn't even look surprised, though I know they were. Considering I hadn't spoken to him at that stage and only knew he was a right-wing lawyer — which was all I needed to know.

We were left alone. He said: "What's your name?" I said: "Libby, and I'm staying the night." At this stage it's crucial not to shilly shally and believe me, boldness is a wonderful thing. I've never had a knockback.

I stayed till six in the morning. Then he said he had to get some sleep as he had a big meeting interstate that day. I don't think you'll believe me if I tell you who with; but now I've gone this far, I will. The Prime Minister. He will never know how pleased I was to hear that. Only Mr. Reagan could have suited me better.

I always enjoy leaving the hotel. This is how it goes: he offers me money for a taxi and I never take it unless I haven't got any and I say: "Goodbye, thanks." and close the door. He's snoring, I bet, before

I get to the lift. I go past the receptionist or whoever is hanging round the foyer, and I feel just great. I don't feel a scrap of shame or guilt, just healed in a way. I'd never change into day clothes, even if I had any with me. It'd look as if I was pretending I hadn't stayed the night and was ashamed. I say "Good morning" to the receptionist, if there's one, hop into the taxi, having a last cigarette on the way home, stinking of sex and feeling utterly pure, simplified and made well again. Don't ask me why. That's how it is.

I haven't got out and got a dose of anything tonight as it turned out. I cooked some artichokes and my daughter and I sat up in bed eating them with butter and lemon. I came in with the tray and found her reading this story. I said: "Mrs. Travers! Reading a story like that! It's not fit for your eyes. Doctor will be shocked." "Well, if you will keep writing pornography Warner, and leave it lying about, what can you expect? You do want someone to read it, don't you?"

# MOYA COSTELLO

### The Party

The women checked each other out and me. Taking sidelong glances during conversation. Whatever it is, I don't measure up to the standard of womanhood.

I wish I'd dressed 1960s revival, in geometric shapes and solid colours. Instead I am conventionally pretty in pink silk. No one here is punk, feminist, gay outrageous, radical or even immodest. They are Katies and Sussan women.

It is Newcastle. It is a party of professionals. Of the two men I speak to, one is a dentist and the other an optometrist. I came with a lawyer. Either they don't come from Sydney, they become straight when they leave, or they become straight when they're professional.

The two hosts maraud the room for the most attractive women to be seen to dance with, grope, speak to. We writhe in slow burn.

Later, women are dripping off the arms of men. It's a formula so standard it's irksome. Anyone vaguely non-conformist has left/is leaving.

I go to the toilet. I sit. I watch. I think, "Yet who would have thought the woman to have so much water in her".

## The Waiting Room

The waiting room at the Gare, Nice.   Platform One.

The neon sign outside — a man in a chair, facing a clock.

The room is oblong. Nothing in the centre. Just chairs lining the four walls. One entrance. A clock.

It is quiet, as waiting rooms always are and people speak in whispers. Yet there is no particular need. No loud speaker announces arrivals or departures;   all the hustle and bustle is at the entrance to the station, before the main information board.

Any arrival causes a slight disruption. Most eyes look up. Except for a younger woman, seated by her lover, for whom idle interest in small things seems rare.

The arrival of a foreign woman causes disturbance. Carrying a pack, being female and alone. Men's eyes linger longer; or the staid curiosity of two old women.

The room is not crowded. No-one is seated next to anyone to whom they are not connected. There is a family, the lovers, an old man with two women, an old woman alone. She is the first to leave. At no significant moment. She doesn't look at the clock. Her expression is wan throughout.

There is also a crazy man. He is mimicking a cat, who has been encouraged by the smell of cheese the foreign woman is eating. His joking is not directed to anyone in particular. Like a crazy person, he is not really eliciting a response. He is involved in his own chatter and the cat.

The lovers are concerned with themselves. He is bland, nondescript. She is irritated with the boredom of waiting. They leave.

The father of the family is amused at the intermittent whispering. The foreign woman's makeshift dinner is entertaining. The son, a solid youth, stares sullenly. The mother has the placated air of house-wifely wisdom. They whisper at intervals to each other. About trains. He checks his watch by the clock. They sigh quietly.

Someone enters. The foreign woman, heady with wine, knocks over an empty cup. The crazy man makes a joke about the wisdom of choice of wine over water. She is perturbed about what to do with the mounting bread crumbs that always gather from French loaves. She senses the disdain of the old crones.

One leaves with the old man. The other stays. After a period she too begins dinner. French bread in a sandwich, neatly wrapped in foil. Crumbs fall, if at all, delicately. The others return with news, perhaps, of timetables.

The foreign woman puts the dinner things away. She concentrates on her movements, the only in the room.

She is cool. She has something to aim for. Steadiness over the influence of wine. She brushes crumbs from her clothes, gets the pack on her back, and picks up her hand luggage in a simulation of co-ordinated movements.

She leaves the room.

### An Imaginary Conversation about Brian 'Squizzy' Taylor

Hey, I must tell you what happened the other day. You know how we went up the coast, um, with this young guy? He was like, ah, a self-styled punk. Yeah. Only about 14. Well, he got involved in London, he was staying there for a while, with these working-class kids; you know, like REAL punks. They wrecked football trains and he got hooked on cough mixture and god knows what, dog pills, gaad. Well he came up the coast with us, to dry out, and its just RIFE with hippes, you know blonde hair, Balinese gear, God. They went CRAZY over Richard Clapton, he had a concert there, when he sang "I've got those blue bay blues", you know, about Byron Bay? I mean, that song must have been written ten years ago.

Well, O God, he wore a heavy German overcoat, like a military one and hobnailed boots, like these great clumping things, and he had black pants, and short spiky hair dyed red, you know. And he walked onto the sand; I mean this is the middle of summer, the proverbial burning deserts. And I thought, WHAT IS THIS GUY GOING TO DO? And then I thought, I mean, what do punks do in summer? No, really. What do you do in black plastic? I mean it's non-absorbent, right? Surely you have to consider these things. Unless, I dunno, punks go in for endurance tests. I mean it's just downright uncomfortable. And black. All that black, it just absorbs the heat. And try to keep looking pasty-faced. They probably raid the chemists for Block-Out. I mean how'yr gunna avoid a tan? Well, you just couldn't go out, could you?

I mean punks are REALLY OUT OF PLACE IN AUSTRALIA, AREN'T THEY? WINTER IS THE SEASON OF THE PUNK. They must have a REALLY HARD TIME IN AUSTRALIA.

Well you'll never guess. I was just looking at the paper the other day, and what do you think? I saw this piece about this Brian 'Squizzy' Taylor, or something, and he's a PUNK SURFIE. Can you imagine that? I mean, it's taken an Australian to do it? Are Australians known for their ingenuity or something? 'Cause this guy's got it. He's won some surfing award or something, you know, like riding a board? He's got these black wraparound sun-glasses and tight pants and sandshoes, and he walks onto the beach like that, I mean ISN'T THAT AMAZING?

It's like, well I think it was an art book, yeah, on Van Gogh, and in it his letters to his brother were quoted, and I remember looking up the references and finding they hadn't been published in English, then, I don't know, a few weeks later a book of his letters came out, in hardback. It's one of the few hardbacks I've bought, I've bought another one I think it was Blood Red Sister Rose, you know, by the Australian guy, um, Thomas Keneally, that's right; or another time I'd seen a programme on Che Guevara and Tanya, his last girlfriend, and then I was just looking at some poetry, in a bookshop and I saw a poem about Tanya by William Carlos Williams, or one of the American women poets, um, Ann Sexton or someone. Yeah, and then I was thinking about how punks manage in Australia and here's this guy in the paper, ISN'T THAT INCREDIBLE?

## Life and Casualty

A REPORT BY THE V.D.U. OPERATORS OF THE MANAGEMENT
OF THE TEMPORARY CODING SECTION.

       As we walk along the street Chris looks up to the neon
sign atop the tall office block to which we have been assigned: LIFE
AND CASUALTY. "God, could you get anything more bizarre!" she
says. We're the casualty. We feel like the walking wounded. The pound
of flesh. Some days we look and feel sick. Fear sends toxins through
our bodies. "No-one should have to do this just to earn a wage",
Lorraine decries.

    Someone like Maria is married to a factory manager who keeps
her on a strict budget. They're buying their first house. She does
the housework and looks after a baby without his help. Before this
job she worked for a dentist who exploited her. Her reaction is to
overcompensate with a schoolgirlish goodness at her work, keeping
her smiles for her bosses. They can do no wrong. It's her defence.
She has to believe that.

    Most of the professionals who work with the computer earn well
over 15,000. One woman owns a flat which she wouldn't think of
living in herself, it's such a hole. She rents it out for $64 a week.
Her brother manages a coffee plantation in New Guinea. Does the
plot thicken? Another woman is looking for a unit. Her limit is
120,000. The real estate agents ask about finance. From the family
she replies. My father's a doctor. A manager says that the more
interesting jobs in the Public Service are at lower levels. But he'd have
to take a drop in salary. About 30,000.

    HOUSING THE CODING SECTION: PART OF A FLOOR OF AN
OFFICE BUILDING WAS RENTED. IT PROVED TOTALLY IN-
ADEQUATE. (1) BROKEN BLINDS LET IN DIRECT GLARE
FROM THE SUN ONTO THE SCREENS. (2) SEATING CONSISTED
OF ORDINARY CHAIRS WITHOUT CASTERS OR MECHANISMS
FOR ADJUSTING HEIGHT. (3) NO COPY HOLDERS. (4) EX-
TENSION CORDS AND DOUBLE ADAPTORS HELD BY TAPE.
(6) NO WORK BREAKS. RESEARCH RECOMMENDS APROX.
10 MINS. REST EVERY TWO HOURS, OR A FOUR HOUR SHIFT.
THE CODERS WERE WORKING A 7 HOUR DAY PLUS OVER-

TIME.

The male supervisor refers to 'getting it up' when we commence work with the system each morning. I feel sick and useless. There's no strategy that springs to mind that I can use immediately. Lorraine explodes. I think about getting him on sexual harassment. But it's all muddy especially when we think he is a gay misogynist. Moreover he doesn't obviously offend all the women. Sharon leads him naively into innuendos. There's feminist theory for female masochism. She goes to the doctor with her husband about her pregnancy. She is too embarrassed to ask intimate questions about sexual behaviour. Her husband isn't. She is shocked at what she hasn't even dared to think about.

Dianne postulates that Sharon is attracted to the supervisor. We can't believe this, and if we do, it still leaves us mystified because we cannot account for it.

IT WAS CLEAR THAT MANAGEMENT WAS NOT CONCERNED WITH THE OCCUPATIONAL HEALTH, SAFETY AND COMFORT OF THE V.D.U. OPERATORS. THEIR CONCERN HAD BEEN WITH THE HARDWARE OF COMPUTER TECHNOLOGY, BUT NOT FOR THE PEOPLE WHO OPERATE THE TECHNOLOGY. THEY HAVE SPENT THOUSANDS TO SEE THAT THE COMPUTER OPERATED IN CORRECT TEMPERATURES, YET THE V.D.U. OPERATORS WORKED IN THE HEAT GENERATED BY MACHINES PLACED IN CLOSE PROXIMITY TO EACH OTHER, WITH AN INADEQUATE AIR-CONDITiONING SYSTEM. ONE CODER HAS WORN SUNGLASSES, THERE WERE INTERMITTENT COMPLAINTS OF SORE EYES, HEADACHES, STIFF NECKS, RESTLESS SLEEP. TIREDNESS AND STRESS.

Dianne worked at a garage for long hours and no overtime. When she discovered she had been consistently underpaid, she told the boss off and left the job. Her husband drives for one of the private bus firms in the Western suburbs. He is personally abused by his boss when anyone makes a complaint about the service. Dianne is the first to work out our pay is wrong and complains about it.

THE TEA ROOM WAS ENTIRELY INADEQUATE FOR ALL THE CODERS TO BE PLACED COMFORTABLY AWAY FROM

THE MACHINES. THERE WERE NO SICK ROOM FACILITIES.
WAGES, INCLUDING OVERTIME AND TEA MONEY WERE
CONSISTENTLY WRONG TILL MID-WAY THROUGH THE JOB.
TEA MONEY WAS NOT PAID UNTIL IT WAS DISCOVERED BY
CHANCE THAT IT WAS DUE TO THE CODERS.

Dianne believes that if you are being paid you are bound to work
to the best of your ability. She is the fastest and most accurate coder.
She assumes employers are honest like herself until it becomes
obvious that they aren't. Tired and stressed at the end of a full day
she fights with her husband at night. The computer programme has
errors that interrupt the smooth flow of her work and waste a con-
siderable amount of her time. She points the errors out to the prog-
rammer and discovers she knows more about the programme than
he does. Why is he earning three or four times her salary?

ONE CODER WAS TAKEN ASIDE BY MANAGEMENT ON
A FRIDAY AFTERNOON AFTER WORKING HOURS. IT HAPP-
ENED TO BE ONE OF THE CODERS WHO HAD BEEN PART-
ICULARLY VOCAL ABOUT SHODDY WORKING CONDITIONS.
THE CODER BELIEVED SHE WAS BEING THREATENED WITH
TERMINATION OF HER EMPLOYMENT. THE ASSISTANT DIR-
ECTOR CLAIMED IT WAS A MEETING TO DISCUSS PROD-
UCTIVITY AND HER "PROBLEMS". HE DID NOT PRODUCE
ANY EVIDENCE TO SUPPORT HIS CLAIM THAT HER PROD-
UCTIVITY WAS LOW AND HER ERROR RATE HIGH. HE RE-
QUIRED THAT SHE SEE A COUNSELLOR. THE CODER ON
ADVICE FROM THE UNION THAT COMPLIANCE WITH THE
REQUEST WAS NOT OBLIGATORY, REFUSED. SHE BELIEVED
IT WAS AN ATTEMPT TO SILENCE HER BY VICTIMISATION
AND HUMILIATION.

Chris and I have had university educations which make us slow
to act and prevent us from clearly seeing to the essence of things.
I recommend further education to Lorraine so that she won't have
to face these working conditions all her life. But she's not sure that
the best thing to do isn't to stay on the shop floor and help fight
in the important battles that always take place there.

Lorraine had courage. I'm full of fear. But I don't know what of.
My fear is irrational. The people who employ me are just that. Though
they are men. If we all stood naked together, we'd be equal. To rem-

ember we're equal. It's a confrontation with power. It's abstract (though I experience it concretely) because I can't put my finger on what it is exactly. They earn a lot more money than us. They're secure. It's also a matter of manners. I have been trained to be polite, but I don't want to be. Politeness is used as a deflator of genuine grievances like threats to your health and safety. We all behave as if we're in a civilised environment. The assistant director has a beard and wears soft, open-necked shirts in cream or maroon.

I begin developing completely inappropriate explanations. The assistant director is a very short man, so he gets into power in a big way, taking out his revenge on the world, but especially women.

Some of the women do not support us. We have a minor success with one young woman. She switches her radio from A.M. commercial to F.M. commercial. These women are the first to grab the few new chairs that eventually arrive in the office. I cannot begin to explain to myself how they think the chairs have arrived.

FOUR CODERS WERE CHARGED WITH DISOBEYING AN ORDER FROM THE MALE SUPERVISOR. THE CODERS DISCUSSED WITH A MANAGER THAT A MISINTERPRETATION WAS QUITE EASY IN THE CIRCUMSTANCES. AT THE TIME THE CODERS ALSO DISCUSSED WITH THE MANAGER THEIR GENERAL DISSATISFACTION WITH THE WORKING CONDITIONS, AND IN PARTICULAR WITH THE SUPERVISOR. HOWEVER AFTER SPEAKING WITH THE SUPERVISOR SEPARATELY, THE MANAGER CHOSE TO IGNORE EVERYTHING SAID BY THE CODERS AND THE FOUR WERE SELECTED OUT TO BE MOVED PERMANENTLY TO THE HEAD OFFICE. THE ASSISTANT DIRECTOR SAID THAT IT WAS PURELY AN ADMINISTRATIVE MEASURE, YET HE STRESSED THAT THE CODERS COULD NO LONGER COMMENT ON CONDITIONS IN THEIR FORMER OFFICE. WHEN THE CODERS ASKED WHY A MORE EQUITABLE SYSTEM LIKE ASKING FOR VOLUNTEERS COULD NOT BE INTRODUCED, HE SAID THAT MANAGEMENT HAD DECIDED TO ACT IN THAT WAY AND NO FURTHER EXPLANATION HAD TO BE GIVEN.

We demand to speak to the director. That's impossible. He walks about the office. You exchange pleasantries or listen to him. But you don't make demands or ask questions. This is an unwritten law like those surrounding gunfights that take place on Hollywood sets in B grade movies. Yet the director walks about the office. We see him.

We speak to the assistant director. Briefly, cramped in his office with a view of the vastness of the city, we behave in a genuinely anarchic fashion. Lorraine calls him a liar. He looks to Dianne for support. She looks away from him to us with a sweeping but silent ooo-wah! At the conclusion Chris makes sure we have our tea-break.

We are successfully isolated from each other in the office. Not one of us is in view of the other. Lorraine immediately turns her buzzer up to full volume. It's a small attachment on the machine that beeps when the pages are turned on the screen. When I can't hear the buzzer I get worried.

I have a friend who is five years old. I talk with one of her parents about how she will adjust to school. She grew up on a small farm where she ran, jumped, dived, kicked, squirmed. I remain seated in front of my machine because I succeeded in school.

Certain things have become clear, like why migrant women are called hysterics when they complain about industrial injury, and why foot soldiers are cannon fodder and nuclear facilities are increasing.

# PAMELA BROWN

## Satisfactory

we have been in town a fortnight. i am noticing everything. the different soft drink labels, the latvian art society, the heat, the plant varieties, the aboriginals. the way everything seems different here, and how, in our new house, i expect my records to sound different and i am selecting music i don't usually listen to.

we've been asked to a party where a local band called 'avant garbage' are playing and we are going to go, but, that afternoon, micky is pulling down an old tin shed in the back yard and she is struck on the skull by a heavy iron pipe, and we spend saturday night at the city hospital.

a nurse takes micky away down a corridor and i try to read some awful stories in rolling stone magazine which they have called 'new fiction'. low grade sexist fuck stories. " 'Pig' was one of his favourite words to describe women, but then I guess it was one we all used. It was a rough-edged time and we were at a rough-edged age and the ones we fell in love with were adolescent Blessed Virgin Marys and the ones we got the clothes off of were pigs." apart from the sexism, i don't like the way the american has written 'clothes off of' so i stop reading.

the corridor opposite the waiting area is dimly lit by purple fluorescence from the side rooms. shiny linoleum and a sign and a few arrows on the walls. a cheerful wardsman pushes a huge tilted bed with an attached steel frame hung with metal chains and triangles. he glides down there and through the doors at the end. the muzak keeps the wardsmen whistling.

there are no smoking signs in the waiting area but everyone is smoking. despite this, i wait for an hour or so before i roll a cigarette.

a large woman, wearing glasses and a mauve uniform, walks over from the reception desk and sits next to me, asks how long i've been waiting. she has a bulbous plastic torch pen hanging around her neck. she tells me they have all worked very hard, been very busy this evening. i strain to read her identification tag to figure out her role here, and say something like "saturday nights must be hectic for hospitals." she says, "oh no, it's not that — we've had nine cardiac arrests," she pauses, "and eight of them dead." this disturbs me but i try to seem casual and empathetic. she continues "nine cardiac arrests in five hours. and then there were the relatives to console." she places her cool hand on my arm and says "of course there's only some people you can tell this sort of thing to." i wonder why she chose me but i say "oh that's alright, i understand, i've worked in hospitals." and i lose her confidence. she stands up and says, in a way that suggests interminable routine, "do you know where the amenities are" naive, and in her care, i reply that i don't. "the phones are down there to the left, just past the coffee and food machines and so on . . .

i think about cardiac arrests. this is when the heart actually stops functioning. the person is dead. i try to understand the attempt to revive these people. the slim faith in immortality. in hospitals the cardiac arrest is THE supreme scientific ritual. alarms sound and everyone drops what they are doing and runs to the revival.

the benches are filling up. a fishbone in the throat case, a man with a broken wrist, a drunken boy with blood on his t-shirt who asks every now and then if he can bludge another smoke. and in the corner an unattractive plump man, who jiggles his legs as he talks, is entertaining three girls with jokes about pregnancy which they find very funny. i roll another cigarette and hope micky hasn't fractured her skull. she did have a gash with bright red blood coming from it. and she has been somewhere down a corridor for nearly three hours. there is more 'new fiction' to read "His date, who looked fifteen even in high heels" and so on, and i decide not to buy rolling stone magazine again.

a fat surgeon dressed in a cap, white gown and operating theatre boots, emerges from the dim purple corridor to talk to one of the people waiting. he has very pale skin, as if he never goes out in the sun. he looks like a butcher. it seems like a cliché but this man really does. it's strange the way people smile when they talk about surgery. he is saying "satisfactory" and letting small grim smiles out through his teeth.

## Back of Beyond

does everybody in this place go home at night disappointed? like i do, tonight.

contrary to john berger, small communities are dangerous.

a tourist raped the young woman who lives in the valley alone. the locals, in the post office, said "that's what happens when you haven't got a man around the place."

the bushfire jumps the road and heads this way. for one day, this brings the people together. the men drive the fire truck, direct the hoses, slap wet hessian bags around. the women make sandwiches and tea.

on sunday afternoon, across the orchard, bob yells to his daughter "run up to the house and get the car deodorant will you."

at work, in the cool room, the plant packer remarks about her neighbour "he's not 'one of those' is he." and i am.

the landscape looks australian. like a grey, yellow and green lino cut of wattle or gum blossom. i think of the sydney skyline seen from the back steps of a house in rozelle.

in the drought lara drives her car out of sight behind her house and hoses it.

the dairy farmer shot rory's dog because it has chased the cows. he dumped the dead dog in rory's kitchen. rory said "it's the most sorrowful thing that's ever happened to me." and he left the district.

back of beyond. gun crazy. old bill says "i'm a conservationist, but it can go too far." he shoots satin bower birds. "they eat the seedlings." my friend and i plant the garden under wire netting.

when jim lays poison for the dingoes he says "it's too bad if your dog takes a bait."

trail bikes and subarus. on weekends you can hear them coming for miles.

# SUZY MALOUF

## Balmain Incidents

1.
        Yesterday, an old woman derro stopped us, me and Dallas, in the street. She said to Dallas, "I want a packet of cigarettes and I haven't got any money. You couldn't give me eighty cents could ya?"

Dallas looked at me for a cue. I just sort of said "We haven't got much money either." And then we both looked at her. She had a round face like a pumpkin with a few sharp, dirty looking teeth in it. Straight dark hair. She was grinning at us.

"We can give you a cigarette," said Dallas.

The woman was looking at her, smiling sort of manically, like we smile at each other, like we smile at a joke when we're stoned.

Then I started to smile and giggle a bit. "I can't cope," I thought and tried to communicate to Dallas by jigging about on the pavement. "I don't know what to do."

"I did want a packet. It's just that I haven't got any money."

When Dallas saw that I was giggling, she gave a bit of a nervous laugh. The woman looked at her all the time and when Dallas giggled, she giggled a bit too.

I wanted to say, "Where do you live? How are you going to get home? Do you have a home? Children? A husband? A life? What sort of life?"

Dallas gave her some money and she said, still grinning, "Are you sure it's all right?"

"Yeah. It's all right." I giggled again. We started moving off. "I can fix you up when I get my pension if it's not all right."

"No, no, it's all right," said Dallas in the friendly way she has.

We walked away. "That'll probably be us in a few years," I said to Dallas, still giggling. But Dallas didn't want to see a joke.

2.

A drunk gave me a lift in a taxi. I saw him as I was walking up to the bus stop. He was trying to stand up in such an uncoordinated way, I thought he was retarded at first. Spastic or something. But when I got closer, I could see that he was just drunk. I sat down on the seat to wait for the bus. I must have broken the ice because he sat down next to me and said, "I'm really drunk love and I wanna get a cab. If you see one will ya stop it for me?"

"Certainly," I replied. He just sort of nodded his head. There's an early opener around the corner called 'The South Pacific'. He must have come from there.

He kept talking. "I'm goin' 'ome. 'Ad enough today. Wanna get a cab to Drummoyne".

"Hmmm," I say in a kindly fashion as one says to small children when one can't understand their language.

"Where are you goin' love?"

"I'm going to Rozelle," I said.

It was his turn to say "Hmmm". Then there was a bit of a silence, but not much.

"Ow long 'ave ya......'ow long 'ave ya lived in Balmain love?"

"Two years," I said sort of proudly. Two years and two houses. I was starting to feel like a local.

"Two year, eh?" He made disapproving clicking noises with his tongue.

"That's not long enough. I shouldn't even be bloody talkin' to ya."

I looked at him a bit quizzically, I suppose. He was looking at me with wide eyes.

"It's all bloody people like you that's destroyed Balmain."

I couldn't keep looking at him all the while he spoke because I had to keep an eye out for a cab. A Porsche drove past.

I know what he means. He means what I feel when I see Porsches driving by while I'm waiting for the bus. He means what I mean when I walk past the trendy shops and spit on the aluminium plate glass windows where lead light used to be.

"It's all them bloody hippies an' flower children....."

"Yeah, I know but....."

"Bloody Hippies."

I didn't get into the rave, that it's not so much the hippies as the bloody bourgeoisie, because the cab came. And anyway, the difference between me, the hippies and the bourgeoisie probably isn't as vast as I would like to think it is.

I stopped the cab for him and said, "Here you go," feeling like I had just done a good deed for the day.

"Can I give you a lift," he said. Just like that, after accusing me of destroying Balmain.

"Do ya wanna lifta Rozelle?"

So I got a lift from a drunk. In a taxi. At nine in the morning.

3.

I walk along that street that has seen half my life played out upon it. I have walked along there, past the pinball parlours and the sex shops and felt at home. Seeing the same faces and the same facades. I have walked along there, my arms about some lover, and I felt like I owned that whole fucking street. And I have walked along there, as I do tonight, in the same alcoholic delirium, the same sexual frustration, that same 'I have to go and catch a bus ON MY OWN now' feeling. And I wish I had one of those old lovers by my side, or a new one. But I don't. I am the independent-woman-about-town.

I get to the bus stop in Druitt Street and inevitably, there is a drunk there, sitting, seemingly waiting for me to come along. Will I write a story about this one? I think not. I am not interested in drunks tonight. I have drunk enough myself tonight. Anyway, this poor guy is really far gone. He is sitting there babbling, absolutely babbling except when he is swigging on his bottle of sweet poison. And I think...all I can think is, "fuck, I wanna go home."

There is a policeman directing traffic between the Queen Victoria building and the Town Hall. A man comes and sits next to me. He looks fairly decent in a semi-trendy sort of way. I take a cigarette out of my bag and light it and sure enough, he says, "Can I bludge a cigarette off you?" He looks at me in a little boy appealing way and I look at him in his fifty dollar jacket and his inoffensive manner and I laugh. I laugh hard and cynical so that it sounds frightening, even to me, and I say, "Sure." I give him one. I say to him as he lights it, "Do you work?" Just like that. "Do you work?" I am still laughing cynically in my head and he knows, this 'nice' Balmain 'trendy'. He knows that if he doesn't give the right answer I will laugh and walk away and spit in his face as I do so. So he takes a few seconds to say, "Well, that's a bit of a leading question," whatever that means. "Yes I do work actually." And I say, "Well I don't. Why are you bludging cigarettes off me then?"

He exhales a lungful of smoke with a frown. "I only smoke when I'm in tense situations."

We've got a right smart arse here, I think, but I am not daunted because I am the independent-woman-about-town tonight. So I say, "Where are you going?" even though I know he is going to Balmain. We are all going to Balmain tonight. All us people who have made it go to Balmain.

"Balmain," he says and I laugh that same laugh. He looks put off all right. But he still wants to chat.

"Do YOU know what's going on?"

"What do you mean DO I KNOW WHAT'S GOING ON???" I know the world is run by ratbags who are going to blow it up within the next three years if that's what he means.

"All these police and flashing lights. Do you know what's going on?"

Get to the point. "No."

"Myers is on fire."

"Really?" I am interested.

"Yes. And there's lots of smoke. Look," he points over the top of the Queen Victoria building, "you can see it, although it's calmed down a lot now, but at one stage there was flames coming out of the top of it."

"Yeah? Gee." I toy with the idea of going to have a look at one of the bastions of capitalist consumerism going up in smoke. But if they've quelled the flames coming out of the top of it, there's not much point really.

The drunk gets up and starts stumbling up the footpath, veering towards the street. He is still babbling. So is the guy next to me.

"Yes, that's what the police are doing. Directing traffic away from Myers."

God, he wants to talk about burning buildings all night.


"Oh I do hope that man doesn't get run over." My sympathies are with the drunk. Thursday night shoppers are laughing and pointing at him. The trendy is indifferent. A 401 pulls around the corner and not a second too soon.

"Here's a 401," I say in my bright, cynical, woman-about-town way.

And sure enough, all these people emerge from the environs of the Druitt Street bus stop, from the innermost gothic crevices of the Town Hall. And they are all going to Balmain. The trendy and I have to wait in a queue while they pay their fares.

"It's disgraceful," I say to him, "they should have a conductor on this bus."

"Yes, but it's late," he says.

"Nevertheless. It's disgraceful, it's Thursday night isn't it. Do you know," I say in a worldly way, "do you know they want to take the conductors off all the buses and just have them driver operated?"

He nods his head.

"Well it's disgusting. Taking people's jobs off them like that."

My last words to Mister Nice Guy. Lost him on the 401. I sit down next to his female equivalent. She wants the whole seat to herself, but will settle for three quarters of it. She has long legs and long blonde hair and long red fingernails. She is actively discouraging me from sitting next to her. So I say to her, in my role as tough-woman-on-her-own, I say to her in a loud voice, "Do you want this whole fuckin' seat lady or can I have half of it?"

It's been a hard night.

# SHEILA ANDERSON

## A Home of One's Own

Mother was in the kitchen, holding forth about some gifted chimpanzees she'd read about, and Dad was pretending to listen while he drank his tea, but his eyes kept sliding back to his newspaper. I was pretty bored. Christmas was over, and the rest of the school holidays offered nothing but work in the orchard — no seaside vacations for us! So here I was, hanging around the kitchen, and half dreading, half looking forward to, the next couple of days when the pickers would be arriving, and the work would begin in earnest.

From where I sat, balancing irritatingly on the back legs of the chair, I could see down the track to the front gate. An old utility was nosing in, towing a huge, spanking new van. As it drew nearer, I could see our dogs yapping hysterically at the big blue heeler who rode in the back of the utility jeering at them. I recognised the dog before I saw the driver.

"Hey, Dad! It's Barney — that's Mike carrying on in the back: and there's someone else . . . "

Dad went out, looking pleased, though of course he and Barney had as usual parted with acrimony and mutual recriminations at the end of last season. According to Dad, Barney had been coming for about sixteen years — years before I was born. I suppose I was about twelve this year, the year Barney arrived with a wife. We heard Dad's voice, raised after the initial greetings and exclamations: "Stella! Come and see who's here!"

Mother patted her hair and cast off her apron before she followed him out, and told me to fill up the kettle and put it on again. She'd always had a soft spot for Barney. "His own worst enemy," she used to say, when he'd have to take a day off to recover from a hangover.

He was always sullen on those days, and we children kept out of his way.

He was a good-looking man, I suppose — he must have been as old as Mother and Dad, but he certainly didn't look it. He'd always been a loner — spent months out in the far west of New South Wales rabbiting, then there'd be the potatoes in Southern Victoria, our place, and then the grapes at Mildura, with only Mike the blue heeler for company. He was a great reader: one of the first things he'd do when he arrived was to browse through the bookshelves to see what was new since his last visit, and he liked to sit around talking about what he'd read.

At some time, he must have become a subscriber to the Readers' Digest, because they were always sending him mail. I remember Mother taking his letters down to him one day. At that time he used to sleep in the back of his utility, and drive into town for his meals.

"Here, Barney," she said, smirking, "here's a record offer that says you can enjoy the grandeur of opera in the privacy of your own home!"

You couldn't have joked with him if he'd been having one of his bad days, though. I'd had the rough side of his tongue a few times, but then, I don't think I ever liked him much, and I don't think he liked me, either.

All the same, I wandered out after Mother. The heat was exhilarating. Summer wasn't old enough to have drained all the fresh green from the trees, but the sun was hot enough to draw out the acrid smell of the peach leaves and the heavy spicy scent of the oleanders that lined the track. The earth was still firm under my bare feet; later in the season, my toes would luxuriate in inches of silky dust which Mother cursed, as every car coming up the drive sent clouds of it billowing over and into the house. Mother used to hose down as much of the track as she could every evening. Sometimes she used to hide behind the hedge and send a jet from the hose all over us when we came up at dusk, riding in the bins on the back of the trailer.

Now she was all gaiety and smiles of welcome as a slim, fair woman, blue-eyed and deeply tanned, stepped out of the utility, and was proudly introduced by Barney as "my wife, Terry." Mother launched into welcomes and congratulations, and told Terry how she had always thought Barney needed someone to look after him, and so on. Barney accepted it all with a proud, fatuous grin. Terry was a cool one, though. I could see by the way her glance went from our old weatherboard cottage to the van that she thought the van vastly superior. However, she was pleasant and self-possessed as she refused Mother's invitation to have a cup of tea, and asked Dad where they'd set up the van.

That van! Apparently they'd only had it for a few days, and Terry was always driving in to town over the next few days to get material for curtains, and stuff like that. She asked Mother up to have a look at it, and Mother was quite impressed. Terry said they'd had a good year, plenty of work, and she'd finally got Barney off the grog. She wasn't going to slave for him out in all weathers, just for him to blue the lot on drink! Not that she didn't like a glass herself, she said, but first things first.

Mother and Dad thought Barney was lucky to have met someone like Terry — a hard worker, good manager and a nomad like himself. She could no more have 'settled down' than he could, and she liked an outdoor life. She had been married before, and divorced: I think Barney had, too, but Dad never passed on any of his confidences.

New Year was coming up, and Barney and Terry talked a lot (or Terry did) about some cabaret evening at the pub that they were going to. Barney had been coming to Paranga for so many years that he had quite a circle of friends, and he was anxious for Terry to meet them all. I heard Terry telling Mother what she was going to wear, when Mother and I took out the morning tea. Mostly I took it out myself, but the day before, I had taken it out to the block where Barney and Terry were working, and although their ladders and picking bags were there, I couldn't at first see them. I was just about to call out when I heard Terry's laugh, and saw them lying together in the long grass. They were making love, and Barney's flushed and rapturous face was close to Terry's mocking, laughing one, but as I stood transfixed with fear and a kind of horror, the mockery died from her face to be replaced by a look of agonized ferocity, it seemed to me, and her thin wailing cry terrified me. My heart pounded with fear lest they should see me watching and, looking back, I think too that I felt a kind of feverish interest that made me want to stay, even though every instinct told me to go. Instinct won, and I went off as quietly as I could. I emptied out the billy and told Mother I'd tripped and spilled it, and when she made some more, I beguiled young Peter into taking it out. I don't remember whether I ever told him about what I'd seen.

Anyway, this day Mother was with me — she wanted to see Terry about something or other — and I hung around furtively looking at

Terry, and trying to reconcile her calm friendliness with the joyful wantonness and sudden passion of the woman I had spied on the day before.

Terry was full of plans. They were to have a celebration on New Year's Day — just the two of them — "Our first New Year together, and the first in our own home." Life would be better for both of them from now on, she said. She had decorated the van, and. had bought flowers.

"I've got a chook thawing," she told Mother, "and we'll have champagne. Barney would rather have beer, but I think champagne always makes a real celebration, don't you?" Oh yes, Mother thought so — though I couldn't remember our ever having had champagne.

We heard the utility starting up at dusk that evening, and I peered out to see Barney and Terry driving off 'dressed to the nines', as Mother would have said, whatever that meant. I went to bed without seeing the New Year in — it was not an occasion we made much of at our place.

New Year's Day was bright and hot. We had friends coming for the day: it would be our last chance to enjoy ourselves before the exhausting routine of getting in the fruit crop began in earnest, and that would last for months.

As usual, Mother had baked in a frenzy of irritable hospitality. She hated cooking, but loved entertaining. Now she was admiring her handiwork.

"Look, Jean," she said to me, "I've made a special pavlova for Terry and Barney for their New Year's celebration. Terry's stove isn't up to the sort of thing. Just run up with it, will you, and wish them a very happy New Year."

I didn't want to go, but I took the pavlova, complete with whipped cream and strawberries, feeling that it didn't look the kind of thing that Barney and Terry would appreciate. I carried it out to where the caravan had been carefully sited under the willow trees, stepped under the canvas awning and knocked at the door. Mike, chained to the drawbar, barked ferociously. I thought I could hear Barney snoring, so I knocked again, feeling foolish and intrusive. I thought I heard someone call out, and taking it as a summons to enter, I pushed open the door.

I could see the celebratory chicken on the kitchen table — it had thawed, all right, and the flies had found it. A beer bottle had been tipped over, and the beer had flowed down onto the floor, but my gaze went beyond the table to the double bed in the alcove. Barney and Terry were sprawled across it, still in the clothes they had worn the night before. Terry was sleeping, breathing heavily, her mouth open, but Barney raised his head when he heard me, and I cringed at the sight of him. His eyes were bloodshot, and a dribble of saliva had formed at the corner of his mouth. A look of rage contorted his face, and his speech was slurred through its violence.

"Get out, you little bugger — what do you think you're doing in here? Can't a bloke enjoy the privacy of his home? Now get out before I throw you out!"

But he couldn't have thrown me out — his head fell back onto the pillow, and he groaned. Terry stirred and whimpered, and I left.

I took the pavlova back to Mother and told her, "Barney's got a hangover like last year, and Terry's got one too. I think they've done all the celebrating they'll be doing for today."

I used to think a lot about that day, and the scene I had witnessed in the orchard, especially at night just before I fell asleep. The scenes balanced themselves and see-sawed in my mind, and I thought of them both with equal fear and repugnance. I told my sister about it years later, and she said she thought it was terribly sad. I hadn't thought of it that way.

Barney and Terry came back once or twice more, but it was never the same between Barney and Dad again. Dad said Terry made trouble, and she and Barney certainly used to fight a lot. Sometimes I wonder if it would have been different if they'd had their New Year's Day celebration. It was a sort of symbol for them, you see: it really meant a lot to them, having a home of their own.

## End of the Season

— Edie looked right through me today — she was real nice
yesterday ....

The women, heads down, knives flashing as they trimmed the fruit,
had learned to talk out of the sides of their mouths like prisoners, and
to pitch their voices so that they could be heard against the roar and
clatter of machinery, if they stood close together. This was the only
job in the whole cannery where it was possible to talk at all, and was
prized and envied by the older women, despised by the young ones.

— Mag, mag, mag, jeez, look at them! Edie'll be after that Ruby if
she doesn't shut up.

Ruby shifted her weight from one varicosed leg to the other.

— Look at those boys, leaning on their brooms — why can't they
empty our bins? If the men had to work like we do we'd see some
drooping lillies by the end of the day. Yeah, and they don't have to
work at home with the washing and cooking and that...

Nobody answered. It was an ever popular theme. The women
treated like slaves, like flesh and blood machines; the men free to move
about instead of standing in one place on the wet cement floor for
hours at a time; the greasers swaggering round the machines where the
prettiest girls worked: it was an old story.

This was a stifling evening. The heat pressed down from the high
tin roof, the steam from the condensers rose in choking clouds, and
the smell of cooking fruit was heavy and nauseous. The women, arms
flying as they sorted fruit from one conveyor belt to another, sighed,
and longed for the whistle to blow for the tea-break. But the machines
worked on, unaffected, energetic and beautiful, going through their
complex rhythms and routines. The cans clattered and glittered endlessly along their races. Everywhere metal pounded and throbbed
and leapt and twirled in splendid terrifying ballet. The fork lifts
sped about the factory floor; steam hissed; fruit was stacked everywhere, waiting to be processed.

— Never eat another peach!

— Best you don't anyway — Edie's watching.

— She's all right, she's fair. But that Mr Roberts! Caught Marlene
pinching a couple of peaches and he said, he said 'Take a couple of
those every day and you'd have enough to do all your bottling at the
cannery's expense!' And Marlene says 'Good idea' and takes another

two. He didn't say anything, but.

Hotter and hotter. Old Whispering Grass streaked up his ladder to check the steam pressure on the caustic tank. The caustic fumes had taken their toll of Whispering, all right. He'd been called Whispering for years, because his damaged vocal chords left him no other mode of speech. This year, though, the men had begun calling him Whispering Grass.

— Watch it, feller, me name's Alf.

He'd never minded being called Whispering, though. Now he clambered down and mopped his forehead. The whistle blew for smoke-o. Everyone rushed for the tea-urns, but the women on the caustic belt had to wait until it slowed down. They sulked importantly as they came last the queue.

— Always us — look, we're going on strike one of these nights. We're just going to walk off and leave the thing going — not as though we ever get any overtime, cheating, that's what it is — wouldn't get the men staying on, and them Eyetalian women, they know what's what, they don't muck about when the whistle blows ....

But the other women didn't like that kind of talk.

— They're real nice ladies, some of those Eyetalians.

The young-Queenslanders sauntered, illegally, outside to the railway line for a smoke. Bikies. The older women had eyed them distrustfully early in the season, but now they were all on good terms. They were cheerful enough, liked a bit of chiacking, and the women enjoyed the bawdy undertones of their jokes.

— Hey, I'm an old married lady, I am — who do you think you're talking to like that?

— That Wayne, he's a nice boy, but the things he says! Well, look at him, taking Marlene's tea over to her — she'd better watch out ....

Pretty Michelle went out hurrying slowly, out to join the men for a smoke, out to enjoy a breath of fresh air and an ego-trip.

— Here she comes, the sex-kitten of the caustic belt!

— C'mon, Michelle, sit next to me tonight!

The fruit boxes were hauled out of their piles and everyone sat around smoking and complaining. Too hot for the usual lively horseplay.

— Hey, Whispering, got any tonight?

Michelle is inquisitive.

— Got any what? What's Whispering got?

— Nothing you'd want, Michelle — he's too old, see. Look, run along like a good girl. We got things to talk about.

Michelle pouted, threw away her cigarette and departed through the door displaying the notice "Personnel not Allowed Beyond this Door. Danger. Beware of Trains". No-one took any notice of this, except when Mr Roberts came on his rounds. He'd had a word or two to say about people going outside in working hours! Instant dismissal. But everyone who wanted a smoke went out there just the same. It was better than crowding into the toilets, and you could always see old Roberts coming a mile off. Him and his mauve nylon shirt. Anyway, so long as that goodlooking supervisor was about, there was nothing to worry about — he'd have something else on his mind. The bikies gathered in a close group round Whispering, smoking with their hands cupped round their cigarettes in furtive economy, until the back-to-work whistle blew.

Two a.m. The shift finished. The caustic belt slowed to a halt and the operators resentfully eyed the clock — eight past two! They lagged up to the factory front.

— Look at them lairs watching us come out. That Errol, he's only been married three months — pity his wife can't see him eyeing off the birds. Reckon he's waiting for Michelle?

But no-one cared enough to answer. Their legs ached, their backs ached, their hands were puffy from moisture and their eyes reddened by the caustic fumes. They punched the time-clock and dragged themselves homewards.

The bikies picked up their old ladies from the pear processing section. Most of them lived together in an old farm house, out of town. Their bikes were huge, wonderful .... even the local women, old hands at the cannery and contemptuous of the bikies and the Queenslanders, would stop and gaze as though mesmerised at the big black machines crouching in the car park.

— Wouldn't mind a ride. Gee, they're nice!

This was Ruby. The others squawked with laughter.

— How'd you get your legs into them boots, Ruby? Can you see yourself in a helmet? How'd you go living in sin out on the Paranga road?

They didn't condemn the bikies and their girls in the same way as they passed judgement on Michelle's flighty ways. Everyone knew about the bikies! Sex laid on — drugs — bashings, too, but they didn't like to think about that.

The hot weather dragged on. The women had another focus for their interest. Barry. You had to admit, Barry had style. Barry didn't lean on his broom: he spent his time wandering from the caustic belt to the pitting machines and the trimming line, talking to the women. He soon picked up the right pitch of speech so that they could hear him. No bawdy talk for him, or chiacking. He asked them about themselves. What their husbands did, and how many children they had, what their interests were. They loved him, and watched jealously to see that he didn't spend all his time with Marlene and Michelle. Got on well with the Queenslanders, and even old Whispering thought he was OK. Told him to call him Alf, though, when he asked why he was called Whispering Grass.

It was right at the end of the season when the rumours started going around. Barry was a member of the Commonwealth Police. Roberts had put him in, they told each other: he was Roberts' spy. But Barry just laughed when they asked him about it.

— Used to be in it once. Not any more. What of it, anyway?

The women still liked him, but the men were wary. Whispering dodged him. The bikies looked at him with narrowed eyes. Long, significant looks. But Barry only laughed.

Michelle wasn't welcome out near the train lines anymore. She didn't care. She was hanging around with Errol, so the Queenslanders could go jump. They always went home with their own old ladies anyway. But the Queenslanders weren't worrying too much about their old ladies. They seemed to be with Whispering all the time. They gave him long looks, too — looks full of deliberate menace, and Whispering scared more easily than Barry.

— No, no more. That Barry, he's on to something. Leave me alone. I haven't got none.

— You have, you know, Whispering. You've been making a good thing out of it with us. Now you be here tomorrow night—same time — with the goods. Hear? 'Struth, the place will be closing down in a few days.

— I got none, I tell you.

The bikies just stared at him — then moved towards him, still staring. Whispering gave a gasp and broke out of the circle. He scuttled up his ladder as the whistle blew. Everyone went back to work.

There was a thunderstorm the next night, and the rain drumming on the tin roof added to the noise of the machines made the floor of the factory almost unbearable. Everyone was tense, longing for the release of the two o'clock whistle, and a breath of fresh air. It had been a long season, and they'd worked every weekend — everyone was showing signs of strain.

Edie was several times seen escorting women to the sickbay, her arms around them in support, their lowered heads and dragging feet exciting concern and interest among the other women. Not as chilling as a real accident, of course, when even before the alarm sounded to stop the machines, the echoed shouts of the men richocheted around the factory, louder and more frightening than the pulsing of the machines.

By the time two o'clock came round, a southerly change had arrived. Everyone shivered, running through the cold rain to the car park in their thin summer clothes. The bikies didn't hurry, though. Waiting for the rain to stop, they said. Their girl-friends got rides home with some of the women from the pear section — saved them a cold wet ride.

Old Ruby was glad to get home to bed. She thought this might be her last season. Thirty five years she'd been going there, and she didn't think her legs could stand another year. If only they'd let you sit down for a few minutes every now and again! And Edie hadn't smiled at her today. Well, she needed no rocking ... It was nearly dawn when she was awakened by the roar of bikes, speeding through the sleeping town. Heading North. Going home, then. Ruby felt a little pang of disappointment. They never gave her that ride they promised. They never even said goodbye. What a shame, going home at this hour in the bitter cold! Should've waited for the end-up night, the barbecue in the car park. Always had a lot of fun that night.

But as it turned out there wasn't any barbecue. Poor old Whispering Grass was found runover — dead on the train tracks, next morning. Must have got careless, everyone said. He of all people should have known when the train was due. And of course, there was the warning notice.

Nobody felt like celebrating the end of the season. Pity, in a way. The cannery closed down a few months later, so the Queenslanders didn't ever come back to the town. It was a dull old summer, the next one, the cannery ladies said.

# ANNA COUANI

**from work in progress**

Talking with another writer. Where are we? What is it we write? And where does it come from? No, what is this area we find ourselves approaching which hasn't been named yet? What is Australian about it?

It's the intensely personal, the intimate, it's production. The production of the most personal-sounding and realistic-seeming work. When you read it do you really think I'm being personal. Do you feel like I do, that no matter how you try and sneak up on it or reveal it, your 'self', what you really are, is always elusive. What is this thing that I am. Is it elusive because it's non-verbal or too complex? Is it like Foucault says, just the question we ask ourselves which is unanswerable and the means by which we're controlled. That we've been led to think it's a question when it's just Life, like that song That's Life, that's what all the people say. That question that religion and quasi-religion answers. Capricorns are very suited to the drudgery of office life, that's why they all put up with it and why I'm a whinger because I'm an aries with aquarius rising and pisces moon. I have no respect for rules. Not that I have no respect for them, I forget that they are there, because I'm so concerned about the self-imposed ethics I'm constantly striving to adhere to. The reason I'm a writer is because of the mercury/moon conjunction, so important in a writer's horoscope. And on the other hand, although groups of people are so important to me, my conjunction of saturn, mars and pluto in leo, directly opposite the aquarius rising makes me a constant, almost impervious and irresistible force for other people, one to be absorbed and reacted against violently, particularly for those neptunian individuals I attract who live out the weak side of my character I can never express, the pisces moon. Does this lay my character bare for you? It seems quite accurate but I still can't make the connection. As though the train's roaring past too fast for me to jump on. Or like the bus stop outside work where my bus, one of my 2 buses, never comes until I've waited for 10 minutes at least. And I always feel, every afternoon, that everyone on the bus stop gets their bus before I get mine. I only live 15 minutes walk from work but I find myself waiting 15 minutes for the right bus, the one that goes about 150 yards closer to home than all the others. Why do I do this? I do it when I feel too tired to walk. I stand on the bus stop in the heat or the cold or the wind, hating it, getting more exhausted by the minute. As well the bus fare seems expensive but relative to what? As well there are never any seats on *my* bus. It seems like an insoluble problem.

## Souvenir

There are some times of the year which seem like anniversaries. As though something is being recalled or relived. There are a whole lot of things I can't face. Then they shake you sometimes without you knowing what they are. Some disturbing event or some change or some loss. A sadness or sensitivity, something picked up, suddenly on the same frequency. I hardly know whether to speak abstractly or specifically. Certain specific things can present themselves but they are not as specific as this general abstract feeling is now, and it can seem to flood in, a series of images connected to each other.

A country and western song is drifting in from somewhere. It is soft enough that I can tell it is a familiar country and western song but not what it is. Just the long drawn out notes, a familiar instrumental run. So I put on a country and western song myself. I want to know it.

The feeling is of being torn or hurt, affected by something. Of feeling passive. The torn feeling is not unpleasant. The music, as so often with country and western, is not extreme enough. It's effective but not satisfying except in as much as it's satisfying to feel something. Then so often I don't want to feel affected by other people so much. I allow them in, receive them too warmly, don't provide a sufficient barrier. The texture of the words changes from the soft sh of sometimes, some thoughts, to harsher sounds, they intrude. There is no story, only a feeling and the feeling is static. It can some back again and again, always the same. The whole story exists for the feeling, the thought, the thing which can bind it together. I arbitrarily choose a story which I remember as clear and static. When I write it, it opens out into specific instances, it becomes chaotic and unclear.It can only work if it is clear now and true for this memory as it appears now. To remember all the things that actually happened isn't the point. But like the country and western song, the record I put on now and listen to, is comfortable and real. The one I heard at a distance is more poignant, more foreign.

I remember a holiday which always had a strong feeling attached to it. The first time I felt I was alone or could go away and leave my family or do anything I wanted. The most significant part of the memory used to be a night on the holiday when I'd taken some morphine and went to see a man I'd met. He'd tried to tell me something but I couldn't seem to understand what he was saying. So the memory consisted of a feeling that if only I'd been able to reach him that night, we wouldn't have separated, he wouldn't have thrown me out and sent me back to Sydney. The memory came back again and again. If only I hadn't been so powerless, if only I'd been able to stay, we could've travelled to Austria and mixed with his sophisticated friends. As I try to remember all the details of the story of this holiday, the intense feeling leaves. The most striking thing I remember about it now is the road which ran across a hill, a dirt road crumbling and eroding from the snow which covered it in winter. Standing on the road at the top of some steps running all the way down the hill to a large building containing shops, you could look straight ahead at the slope of the opposite mountain.

But when I think of that story I only think of the physical memory now. The feelings don't seem to affect me anymore. I remember it as though I was there alone, as though I didn't realise how alone I was. The man I met contacted me, months later back in the city and seemed a terrible person. But still for years after that, a poignant memory persisted.

I am lying on the side of the pool now. I look across the extremely neat laid out paths, lawns and flower boxes between the stark white units. Beside me a blond woman wearing a pale blue bikini of the same type as mine is talking to a foreign man. He is telling her about his plans to become a musician. She is speaking to him in a very correct way. Yes, that is all very well, but, you see, musicians must be people with a great deal of talent, and they must work hard. It is not only a way of enjoying yourself. Yes, he says, but I think you are not understanding what I say. I do not mean that. They are sitting very close together.

Beyond the walls of the garden is the bay. I can't see very much of the water. The opposite shore is industrial and there is noise from machinery and traffic, quite loud. Beyond that, the harbour bridge and other buildings, more misty. The noise of traffic is loudest but I can only see traffic which is higher than cars, − buses and trucks, moving past a small section where there are no buildings.

The memory of lying here several years ago becomes like a substitute for the memory of the snow country in summer. It is much closer, and only a few hundred yards from where I live now. But the strongest memory is of talking at length with friends, not the affairs. Hour after hour at the swimming pool looking over the garden to the view enclosed by the block of flats. Gradually getting hotter and hotter until the only thing to do is jump into the pool.

The memory of the snow country melts away and melted away as I remembered it. For the first time with understanding. There is a story which is no longer touching for me but which has such striking elements of alienation — you are a foreigner, the woman who runs Katies got on so well with Alexi. Is she jewish. I ask Alexi. No, they have a rapport because they're european, Katie isn't jewish. A fish out of water, how appropriate to be in snow country for the summer, having an affair with an austrian ski instructor who's working as a brickie's labourer. And for the first time I thought I may never have to go back to the family again. Here is a man who travels the world who could take me with him.

The personal nostalgia and pain disappears when I see — that's what it is to be foreign. Of course it was easy to think of turning my back on a career I could never really have on the terms I imagined as a teenager entering university. Once back in the city, the austrian ski instructor looks so much more like a man who abuses women. What an excellent vehicle for all these hated oppressions the fiction could be.

## Tail Lights

Many of the shots were taken up on the roof of the building in the
city, looking south over the suburbs, through the smoke haze, and
from a height of a few hundred feet. Each one is nondescript. Like
a series of stills from a boring TV show, ruined even more by snow
on the screen. But one time I stood in a half completed office block
in the plant room at sunset. The internal space was as big as a large
picture theatre and had 12 feet ducts winding about it. Looking west
across the harbour towards where I lived and beyond for miles, to the
edge of the city in the west. The water was golden. You had to be
touched by the scale of the city, by the feeling of thousands of
activities, by the industry, the smoke, by the harbour and the boats.
The year Sydney became a city, the year of uncontrolled land specul-
ation and overseas investment in towers to remain empty for 20 years.
The year to see a hundred cranes on the skyline. For the first time a
feeling, we are living in a city like they do in England, Europe,
America. We could relax.

And now, such sadness.

Hello, how are you. Haven't heard from you for a long time but I
imagine you aren't actually avoiding me. Things have been amazing here
too, though more in that mad sort of way. Everyone's very depressed.
I won't bore you with a why or wherefore, not because I don't want
to, but because I really don't know why. It's as though it's been put
in the water supply, all-pervasive and mysterious. Whenever you go
to speak to someone about how bad you feel, they say, My god I'm
depressed. Are you too? Yeah, what a year. But it's supposed to be a
good year, the year of the serpent. The chinese think serpents are ok,
maybe they're not so good for westerners. I think I feel trapped by
circumstance or circumstances, lots of them. That's the horrible thing,
whenever you think about just one of the dreadful things happening
to you, it seems only a part of it, you can hardly pinpoint something
long enough to attack it. They're on all sides. Paranoia flourishes.
Oh, why don't you think of coming back, don't I make you home-
sick?

The tail lights of a car are speeding away. Malcolm Fraser is still in
power. It's the year of the serpent. A good year but a year of looking
back and reviving rock and roll. Maybe there's a cycle and we're in
for yet more sadness. The countryside looks unreal, we can't look

at it now and think, Peace and Love, we only think, Once I looked
at the countryside and thought, Yes, Peace and Love. We look at the
sunset and remember that we used to say, Look at the sunset.
The red tail lights of another car are speeding away. We are on an
expressway. It is beautiful at night, black. The dash light is reflected
in the windscreen, round and pearly. The speedo has never worked
and the number of miles registered is 0000000. We are playing tapes
of old rock and roll numbers.

## Xmas in the Bush

Running along far away from the road. Along the shallow creek bed,
the wide flat rocks just below the water, creamy brown. The creek
is wide here and open for hundreds of yards until it makes a turn.
And straight ahead above the blackberry bushes and foliage along the
water's edge is the typical country house with a row of yellow pines
up one side, white walls and a red roof. The mother, the father and
the children are here. With friends. The adults stand on the beach
made of river stones or on the big rock in the middle of the creek or
on the bank, talking, talking. All day. They make sandwiches while
they talk. They smoke cigarettes. They point at things. The sight of a
parent's eyes following the pointed finger across to the bank on the
other side of the creek or into the branches of a nearby tree. They
gesticulate sometimes. The men put their hands in their pockets and
take them out again. The women fold their arms or put their hands
on their hips. They go for a walk very slowly while they talk. Along
the road, across the ford, up the hill, round the corner. They stay
away for hours, talking. The shadow of the hill falls over the creek.
It grows cooler. They come back and organise dinner while they
talk. The women talk to each other. The men talk to each other.
The men talk to the women. They all talk at once. They set out the
card table under the trees, light the kerosene lamp and play 500
while they talk. They miss tricks while they talk. The children go to
sleep in the tents and wake up in the night and hear them talking.
Then later they wake up and everything's quiet.

In the morning the father throws the dog in the water. The dog
paddles madly to the shore. The father talks about snags in the river.
They all discuss the difference between snags as in water hazards and
snags as in sausages. Sausage dogs. Smoke. Children who've drowned.
Bushfires. Snakes. Carpet snakes. The long grass. The blackberry
patch. The tar baby. Was there such a thing as Brere Bear. The Pyjama
Girl. Bullrushes. Flash floods. Flying foxes. The hazards of flying
foxes. High tensile wires and electricity lines. Broken electricity lines
hanging down into creeks. Fords with cars on them washed away in
flash floods. River snakes. March flies. Bot flies. The difference
between bot flies and sand flies. Maggots in sausages. Maggot stories.
Meat safe stories. Ice chest stories. Milk delivery when milk was in

pails. The bread cart. The sound of the bread cart. Draught horses. Old draught horses. Horses being sent off to the blood and bone factory. Horses in the city. Sewerage. The sewerage works. Polluted creeks. The correct drinking sections of creeks. The aeration process. Stagnant water. Boiling the billy. Billy tea. The Billy Tea brand name. The inferior quality of Billy Tea. Swaggies. Gypsies. The cleverness of gypsies. Poverty. Bread and dripping. Sausages. Home grown vegetables. Out door toilets. Improvised toilet paper. The long summer nights. Mosquitos. Marshes and bogs. Moonee Moonee and Brooklyn. The possibility of a mosquito breeding in the dew on a leaf. Playing the comb. The mouth harp. The bush bass. Bottle tops. The corrosive qualities of Coca Cola. Big business. Monopolies. Bigger and bigger monopolies. Free enterprise. Russia. The idea of women working in men's jobs. Suez. American election campaigns. The Klu Klux Klan. The colour bar. The Iron Curtain. The Cold War. The ideals of communism as distinct from the practice. China. Industrialisation. Cuba. Atheism and agnosticism. The idea of supreme being. The Church in Russia. The Jews. Israel. The world wars. The next one. The fatalistic approach. The end of civilisation. The end of the human race. The inexorable continuation of the universe in spite of the human race. Humans as microscopic and trivial beings. The frailty of humans. The stupidity of humans. The innate badness of humans. Animal life and animal's code of behaviour. The rationality of animals. The fowls of the air and other biblical quotes. And now I see as through a glass darkly.

At the end of the last hand of 500, they remember other discussions they've had and that they always conclude with politics. The father turns down the tilly lamp.

# WENDY MORGAN

## Where the Tale Takes Off From

No, it's not really a subject *I* could write about. You might be right; perhaps every Aussie *has* got a real sizzler of a barbie story to tell — I suppose it just shows I'm not the genuine article. Kiwis not being sure if you spell it with a c or a q. So they couldn't trust themselves to spit a Canterbury lamb. Besides, mint sauce doesn't hold a hamburger together — doesn't have the congealed-blood thickness that tomato sauce does.

Of course, plenty. But mainly the hybrid sort. Cross between a garden party and a things-go-better-with-Coke affair. Like the people there. You know, goggle-eyed lecturers out of water, students on parole — the sort of crowd you always find at those academic dos.

Well, in a sense there's always plenty goes on. You could gossip endlessly about all the predictables — oh, like Lydia standing too close in that way she does when she whispers about her menstrual cramps — all hush and giggle — or Harry arriving half-drunk, and his lip getting longer and wetter as the afternoon ditto. But when you've seen through so many of these occasions, they all come to look like, oh I don't know — a pound of sausages. Same shape, same pasty texture, and if you prick them they burst messily all over the place.

Not what you'd really call *un*predictable. Unless you count the time when Robbie walked backwards into the Butlers' pool — trying to do an after-you-ladies soft-shoe shuffle for some pair of dowagers. But in a way that was as predictable as anything. And besides, you couldn't make that the high point of a story.

Oh, overly sensational, perhaps. Too easy to make it into a superficial tale. Backyard gossip cleaned up with a bit of acid for the coffee table. I mean, how are you going to capture poor Robbie's thoughts — bubble bubble — as he comes back to the surface and meets all those faces gawking politely? Yet if you don't it's just too slick. The custard-pie-throwing barbie story.

No, of course it doesn't have to end at that point. You could *start* by plunging in with Robbie. Then you could recapitulate — explain how he found himself there, but that seems a bit wet, drifting back to the shallow end. Sorry. I mean it's a cheap trick, really.

Or else you could go *on* from that point. Haven't you always wondered how they cleaned up after the custard pie? Or who spoke after the famous last words? You know, who first blows their nose and suggests a nice cup of tea.

Yes, you could. That way you'd let the party itself give you the form. Beginning, and ending, fixed for you.

Do you mean you could play around with the ritual aspect of the occasion and let it provide a kind of structure? It'd have to be a rite that doesn't work, though, because no one's sure what it's supposed to do (burnt offerings to make the herds multiply, perhaps). And their private thoughts are so much at odds with all the public display, sharing chatter and chops.

Now we're onto something. That's precisely the problem.

I *can't* write about Robbie, fond as I've become of him. I still can't get into his skin, even now, and I certainly couldn't have heard his thoughts then, for all the static. Too much to watch and listen to all at once.

For instance, you'd need to see how Bruce rushes to help — pure reflex — all eager hands. And how many follow his lead, reluctant. Sluggish. And the sneer on Gavin's face — the way his mouth drops open in triumph and delight before he can hide it. And how Dorothy can't handle it at all — turns away and pretends she hasn't seen.

And then you'd have to get into *her* thoughts. There'd be a tacky mixture of embarrassment for Robbie, and annoyance at the way he's made such a mess of her tidy party, and an idea that if she doesn't look, it won't be so shameful for *him*, and therefore not so disturbing for anyone else, especially her.

And so on, endlessly. But as I say, that's not what I want to write about. All right, let's wipe that one. See if we can start somewhere else.

Well, I'll try that same occasion. But I'll just give you a bit of what *I* noticed and thought, and you see if there's anything there that can be worked up into a story. O.K. Once Upon A Time.

Mind you, it isn't exactly a barbecue. It's an academic lunch party. Safari suits. Jewellery. Splaydes. Clever mid-Eastern food, so novel it isn't even ethnic.

Oh, there's a barbecue in the corner of the brick-paved court, discreetly doing shashliks and marinaded drumsticks in foil. But everyone's got their back to it, and no one's licking their fingers. They're not admitting there's grease around. Though I can see it standing on the sweaty foreheads of the men and round their wives' throats.

I'm standing in the passage (it's a terrace house, where the hall leads directly from front door to back) where there's a cool breeze. I can get my back to the wall, so I don't have to confront too many people at once. Certainly feel edgy.

(This is an arrival story: the Butlers were putting on the party to welcome us to the department. But it could just as well become a departure story.)

You know that Bill came originally just for the year under that exchange fellowship scheme. And of course, I came, under my own steam, to do graduate research. Both from the same place. At the same time.

All right, introductions. Prof. Butler steams up with a faceless young man in tow.

"Jan," he says, "I'd like you to meet Jamie Roberts, he's our Joyce man. Jamie: Jan Palmer."

"Hello," I say, breezily. "But actually I'm Jan Dark." (Silly old codger: he knows I go under my own name now.)

My divorce came through just before we left Auckland. And I wasn't going to take my ex in my luggage with me. Thought I could drop him like a dead weight along with his name. We really had faith in change, those days, didn't we?

Anyway, Jamie pushes his photo-grey specs closer to his eyes. The light bounces back at mine, so I can't tell how he's looking at me. Wild surmise? I *can* see the little smirk on my prof's face. Paternal tolerance at a flighty woman's whims. *My* name hasn't registered with him. So presumably he thinks I'm just borrowed from my husband's department. To light Bill's lamp of learning.

Anyway, old Butler's wife gets it right. Very right. Pointedly.

"I'd like to introduce you to Jan *Dark*," she says, bringing up a plump wombat. "Jan's here to do research on triangular relationships in twentieth-century fiction."

It's all too neat. She doesn't believe her pat little formula either.

The other woman, the one I'm being introduced to? I remember she's got an undercooked drumstick that she's trying to carve with a fork and the paper plate keeps bending under all that sawing.

"Are you settling in all right?" she asks. "Won't take you long once you've got a place of your own. I don't think any woman's comfortable till she's set up house, and got her pots and pans in place. Look, if you're having any trouble finding a particular grocery line or that sort of thing, do give us a ring, won't you? Only too happy to help out in any domestic way. Can't offer to help with your research though."

I think she laughs a little here. But she doesn't catch my eye. She's just noticed how I've tied my hair back with a leather thong. You remember how I used to wear it then — long and straight. Wash-and-wear.

And then what? Well, obviously I ease away from *her* as soon as I can. But all through the afternoon, from time to time I catch her watching me between other people's backs. Staring, actually. I think she'd like me to do something silly. Smash a glass. Or get blind drunk, start feeling up one of the men.

Yes, I'd have to say something here about the way I feel. They're trying to corner me. Make me play the part they've cast me for. And the worst of it is I let myself. Like with this woman. She chatters on about the price of furnished housing, the cheapest supermarket chain, that sort of thing. She assumes I'd be shopping for two.

And I talk right back, faking interest. Letting her think I'm just as dedicated as she is. Well, I'm angry of course, at feeling obliged to act so fake. And even worse, I'm too polite to show her I've got more on my mind than she has.

That's the way it goes the whole long afternoon. You notice a lot of irrelevant details. Like this man who's systematically stripping all the leaves off the branch at his elbow. And there's another man whose eyebrows waggle — how ridiculous — at the end of every sentence. And one woman can't stop collaring her little boys whenever they come within reach and patting them on the head. I don't know who she thinks she's reassuring.

But you don't want a catalogue of details like that, do you? I'd need to give you some idea of how the afternoon gets stickier, and everything wet seems to flow together. People sweat, and the glasses sweat, and the wine makes all the edges of things dissolve and the pastries and coffee sog in their cardboard containers.

Everyone's stomachs too full of gas and grog. And my mouth's dry — not from any dry wit, but from talking too much and saying too little. My smile-muscles ache. Through grinning politely when someone's talking at me. And grinning politely when no one's talking to me. Leaning my weight on one leg, then the other.

Well, I'd want to say something about the other women there, wouldn't I ? And how we size each other up.

Like the fledgling graduates. They're not going to be impressed by my academic record, or my years, you can tell by the aggressive angle on their elbows. And the way they chat to each other about their friends without bothering to put me in the picture. They're not sure where I fit, but I'm obviously way off their base.

And then there's Kate. Only woman on the staff at the time. Now *she* impresses me. Tall, powerful build, afro, massive earrings. Massive ego to match. She drops some businesslike chat into my lap — I'm perching insecurely on the end of a banana lounge by this stage — and I fumble around to offer her an acceptable answer. Something wry, to show I've got it all beautifully under control: this barbecue, the thesis, life, the weather, myself.

Yes, I know I am. But type-casting's almost inevitable, when we 're all asking *who are you.*

Well, they're asking too, but in a somewhat different way, of course. Take Philip, for example.

I'm wearing a kaftan, with black embroidery round this deep slit down the front. I've pinned the opening together a little with that badge I had made from a boy scout's belt, that says Be Prepared. He can't keep his eyes on my face. They keep flicking down to it. He's wondering how I mean it to be read. He asks me about Bill's place, and mine, in the Auckland set-up. It's not what he wants to ask, at all. Out of the corner of my eye I see his wife watching through a hedge of people. It's the super-shopper. She can see he's the right distance away from me. But she can't see that his eyes are much more familiar. I can see them licking round my collar bone. But all I can feel is the sweat trickling between my breasts. I can hardly stuff my hanky down there in front of him.

Well, you're right. There I go again. But that's the way it *was*. Or rather the way I thought it was. Actually, this is where Robbie comes in again. Because he was the only person there who really saw me and heard me, for what I was...

Yes, I know. I get to the point of it all, and then words fail me.

There was a — oh, a kind of receptive warmth about him.

Not so much in what he said, as I recall. Put it on paper and it'd sound very ordinary. No, the whole interchange was much more complicated than that. And it wasn't the brilliance of his eyes either: I was too busy holding myself on guard against anybody's charms to be impressed that way. Even if his eyelashes were curlier than anyone else's.

Oh, we talked about a whole lot of things: macrobiotics — he'd been vegetarian for years already — the I Ching; Beckett — he was running a course on ex-patriate writers — where you could hear the purest folk music in town, all that sort of thing.

Well, that was about it, in fact. (This was all after the big splash, by the way.) We just sat there and talked while Robbie's clothes dried out. We plucked at the grass, and chewed on the stems, and leaned on our elbows. And kids barged around us. Then more kids came along, sent by Dorothy: she wanted them to pick up the paper napkins now that the gully winds were coming up.

And then finally Bill peers under the bushes.

"O.K. lamb chop," he says.

I smile apologetically at Robbie and he shakes his long curls out of his eyes to smile back. Bill's come to claim me.

But as they say, that's another tale.

## Exposure

I've come a long way, to see myself reflected in the famous picture window at the Cook hotel. So I don't mind acting the tourist for once. After all, it may be years before I come back across the Tasman again, though the relatives are always urging me to return home. Tempting, to be enfolded once more in the bosom of the family now that I'm a single mother and the girls are still so young. Just have to see if I can make it home after all this time.

There: camera's set for my mother to take me. Next, adjust my smile. I trust its cool irony says I have these tourist gimmicks wonderfully in perspective.

"Ready!" she cooees, and catches me with the mountain looming over my shoulder, mirrored in the glass, while I gaze at the original looking stand-offish behind her. (No wonder. Will the real Mt Cook please stand up?)

So we've arrived, at last, and the fact's recorded. Next: to enjoy the holiday we've been planning for so long. Mother and daughter, and my daughters. We're to be so cozy together, sharing a room. Must unpack all our baggage.

Towards evening, the four of us pass that window on our way to dinner, on the other side of that reflection. It's like being backstage behind a screen. Now that the sun's withdrawn, the peak lacks solidity, like a poorly lit slide. Much less imposing than the warm bustle of the dining room, its tables in orderly ranks. Once we're seated round the square whiteness of our cloth, the soft light it casts is footlights for our faces.

"— It does set off a meal so nicely, all this silver and linen," my mother murmurs, glancing brightly round at the dimness beyond. "Makes a real occasion of it," — which she can't rise to, for all her smiles of appeal. The red menu seems to drain the confidence from her look. She fingers a fork.

"Let me play the hostess tonight," I offer. Trying not to let my impatience show I scan the wine list. " — I wonder if they can turn on a good Australian white. Let's see. And what about the crepes alpines to begin with . . .?"

My air of casual sophistication isn't reassuring her. All the same, the act is for her as well as for the table next to ours, where a gesticulating middle-aged American has a confident grasp of her male friend's attention.

I drop my glance. It falls to my wrist and the heavy chain bracelet Rich gave me for our tenth anniversary. I know I shouldn't wear it still, but it's so elegant. Twisting it further up my forearm I wonder, with a glance around, if I'm making any impression in this room. I can't see myself reflected in others' faces except my mother's, and I don't know if she understands the message in my gesture and clothes (so modish the style hasn't reached here yet).

I turn to pat her hand across the table. The gesture's overplayed. God, she must find me patronising.

"What a treat to be here with you . . ." I enthuse — then busy myself cutting up the food the girls don't want. Such a hammy performance. Intolerable.

The starch is making the girls prickle, and they start pinching each other. I offer low threats with sweet reasonableness in my face and voice. They believe neither words nor looks, but are easily persuaded to visit the toilet. I watch their receding backsides, rounded buttocks wiggling in their tightly fashioned overalls, innocent of their allure. But the adolescent waiter, I noticed wrily, had responded to their gleaming freshness with jokes and choice tidbits.

My mother's gaze follows mine.

"I must say I find these modern tomboy rigouts hard to take," she remarks. "Not really flattering, even when they're straight down below." I cross my denimed, booted legs.

"Well, I don't want to turn them into pretty little misses too young," I say defensively. "They'll be fully fledged females soon enough, all bright feathers then. "

"Yes," she sighs. "How quickly they're growing up. Makes you see your own life slipping away. Still, you never die completely when you have children. Look at your Lindy — could be Nana come to life all over again. I do agree, though, you don't want them growing up too soon. *You* were never that way inclined. I had to hold you down and *tell* you where babies came from before you went to school — you never asked. Simply weren't interested."

Her voice carries such pride in my innocence. Mama mia, if she knew my life now: two lovers on the go and an abortion last year.

"Oh, I tell the girls everything about the facts of life too," I say, fingers weaving a cup. "Abortion, contraception — I handle it naturally, as a matter of course. That's the best way."

She won't match my insistence, looks with careful lack of expression into her fathomless glass. But the corners of her lips turn down. My conviction mingles with wine and defiance.

"You simply can't assume the old standards any more," I argue obstinately. "Those two won't be virgin when they marry — if they ever choose to. The old rules don't apply these days."

"*You* never had any thought of that sort of thing," she protests indignantly. In all our travel together this is the closest we've come — to confrontation. The children are our only point of contact — and sex our point of division. I try to find a path we can both take.

"Were Nana and Grandad happily married?"

"No, they weren't suited: she was oversexed. So was my sister Daisy: she had to get married, you know. Terrible business — she was always running after the boys. Even being a married woman didn't make her any more steady. It nearly broke my mother's heart."

I make a feeble effort to distinguish between promiscuity and responsible choice, then I trail off into a silence to match hers.

\* \* \* \*

Images from this afternoon suddenly flick past my inner eye. I am striding up the Hooker Valley in the snow, each crisp bite of my cleated boots feeding my pleasure. Wayside seats can't tempt me while my energy's flowing free. Under the even sun hay-scents rise from grassy islands and glittering icy granules dissolve into the smooth glisten of water. I fill my lungs with that clear expanse, delight in my arm-swinging vigour. The girls are far behind at our picnic spot where I've abandoned them to my mother. I've resolved to follow this track to its end where they say there's an unmatched view of Mt Cook.

Details of the view imprint themselves, sharp and solid, on my eye and mind: great black boulders *do* nothing yet convey elemental assurance; beyond, the mountains' stillness, while enfolding purple, is the same contained strength. Not intimidating: their unmoving distance makes no demands on me, and I won't find myself reflected here — no mirroring pools in the river, all turquoise clatter. When I cross the bridge I breathe out in long relief: such a chance to act just myself. Thank God, no call to react.

But the mountains *do* change quickly after all. Those ridges, sharp just now for all their paleness against the sky, are dissolving into mist. What my mother, with all her amateur oil-painting authority, would call finding and losing an edge. She knows the rules for turning a postcard snap into a work of art. I can't feel any such certainty. I frame up the mountains in my camera lens but can't take them in: they're as panoramic as a fold-out tourist brochure, and I can't find the angle to encompass them. And when I see those peaks through the viewer their purity looks clichéd, too much like photos of themselves. I lower my camera with a frown, try instead to capture the tangling shadows a matagauri throws over a snow bank.

In any case, time to press on. Time and distance are hard to judge out here in this broad valley. I stride on, pulling ever further from my base. No hint of a look-out point. I tramp on hard for another half-hour and round a large spur. Still no guide-post. Anxiety begins to ooze into my exultant determination like the snow melting into my socks. No way of telling how much further my goal is, let alone if it'll measure up. I allow myself another fifteen minutes to find some sign, another fifteen beyond that as my outside limit. An edge of haste cuts through my rhythm, makes me slide, stumble. Tiredness begins to nag, but I can't afford to relax my pace. Absurd to turn back now, so near my goal, and waste all my energy and my mother's. I *will* get there, if my limbs will carry me.

— But what if the girls break a leg, or get lost, and my mother can't cope alone? Will they think I've had an accident, or missed the track, I've been away so long? The thought chills me. And if they quarrel while I'm not on the spot to smoothe ruffled feelings? Or panic because I've abandoned them?

Suddenly I wheel round, as if a reflex nerve has been struck. No help for it; I can't go on. I'm deflated, and only annoyance fuels my pace. It leaves me no desire to enjoy the snow at my feet or the scenery beyond. I keep my eyes on the clean tracks I'm negating by stamping a reverse imprint. Insane to let myself be so defeated by the power those three have over me.

When, out of breath, I finally slither through the bushes into the picnic hollow, the girls' red parkas are filling it with bustling purpose. Thank God there's been no trouble. My mother's organised them into building a snow house. The walls are only a foot high, but their domestic belief's unshaken — until I step over a bedroom wall.

"Oh Mum you can't," they wail, "you've got to use the *right* door."

Why didn't I keep faith with the rules of make-believe? And why couldn't I trust them to manage without me? A spasm of guilt jerks across me, and then a memory spurts up, uncalled, how Janie or Kay and I used to play mothers cosily together as she sat with her wool and needles, weaving over us a warm cover of approving glances. That memory has a sticky sweet taste I've forgotten in acquiring more astringent preferences. It's a treacle I don't want to be trapped in. So I busy myself with camera focus: a candid shot, to freeze this moment for the girls. (Unposed, they still act the part: Lindy nags at Kate not to track dirt across the floor.) Maybe this'll fix it for their own memories one day.

As I pan through the viewfinder my mother comes into focus, in her spread thighs the solid assurance of a terracotta earth-goddess. She meets the sun's full glow with equal certainty. It perturbs me. But it's admirable in a way. I'd like to capture that. So I frame her up – and snap her sagging dumpily on a low wooden railing, feet stumped in the ruffled white, off-centre with nothing for balance at the other side. The sharp light throws a net of wrinkles over her squinting grimace.

It's illuminating but hardly comforting. I can't find the right image – there are too many unfocussed feelings. She looks pathetic. And strong. And vulgar. And ages old. And fragile. That's what my film's recorded. I feel the shame I did once when I caught sight of her sponging naked, her intimate folds and motions exposed to my reluctant gaze. Better give her a chance to choose a pose for herself. So she stands in the centre of the picture, each arm possessively round a demure grandchild, her smile saying: it's real, and worth noticing, because I'm here looking at you.

\* \* \* \*

In the centre now, between us, is this white square, crumpled napkins and empty cups ranging across it. No linking arms across the vastness, no auld lang syne, no ritual to satisfy us the occasion's done. We leave the dining room feeling vaguely disappointed. The evening's not done, and we can't think how to fill in the time till bed. I've forgotten how to play crib, and reading's too private – we're supposed to be enjoying each other's company while we can.

I suggest a walk. Once we're out of doors, though, the cold scours our lungs, there's no light to see by and the wide asphalted parking bay is an exposed and featureless plain. Nowhere to go but back towards that impersonal light and warmth. Out here the hotel seems the only thing that's real. Beyond it the mountains are merely the flat negative where the stars don't glitter. In any case, we're watching our feet and hardly look up. I feel I should hold my mother's arm to guide her but it's as much as I can do to give her shoulder a brief pat.

Once through the plate glass doors I find it hard to catch my breath in the odour of public carpets. It's little better in our room. Our cases and bric-a-brac — talc, disprin packet, hairbrush, tickets — sprawl uneasily over the dressing table. We don't talk: "Mustn't disturb the girls, they need all the sleep they can get, don't they look like angels, you can tell they're dreaming sweet dreams, how lucky children are. . . ."

I want to get into bed and swaddle myself in its blankets, in a hurry to take off my clothes and shuffle off the day. So while my mother's still undressing in the adjoining room I have the bedcovers up round my face like a shawl. Through half-closed lids I can see her framed in the doorway and lit from within, lifting her jumper carefully over her hairdo. She looks so awkward and weary I want to leap out, do it for her — anything rather than look at this old old woman sagging in her petticoat, face fallen in sour creases. But it's a distance I can't cross. She's so slow — how could she have got so feeble? I don't remember her like that, won't relate this strange old crone to me. I'd rather not watch, but she doesn't know I can see her, and my movement, if I turn away, might catch her attention. In recoil I close my eyes, but not before a last image imprints itself on the black of my lids: elbows angled, she fumbles behind her back and then frees her empty swinging bags of breasts from her bra. I hug my arms tight round me to protect myself against that horror.

# ELIZABETH JOLLEY

## It's About Your Daughter Mrs. Page

Dear Mr and Mrs Page,

I am sorry to have to write to you again though I realise that since you haven't answered my other two letters you don't particularly want to hear from me.

It's about your daughter Mrs Page. I'm sorry, but I don't know what to do. My problem seems so big I don't know what part of it to start writing about first. It probably goes all the way back to when we first came to this country when Donald was six years old and he was so sure he could see his granny down there on the wharf waiting to meet him off the ship at Fremantle. We kept telling him grandma was back home in her house. She wouldn't come, you see, she had lived all her life in the same street in that tall narrow house of hers in the Black Country. She just wouldn't come with us and Donald missed her terribly for years, specially when Betsy, his big sister, went off and married the wheat belt.

Of course I'll skip all that lot and come to my worry about Donald and your daughter Pearl. You must understand I am very fond of your Pearl, she is easy to love and she is very determined in her relationship with my son. She accepts our home and family life as easily and naturally as if it were her own home. I realise that because you are travelling in plastic and having to move from one country to another you decided quite wisely I think that Pearl should stay in one place and go to boarding school. You chose a respectable college for girls so Pearl would have the privilege of a sound education and a good upbringing. Boarding schools seem so big these days and when the girls have problems, I don't mean things like French or arithmetic, I mean personal difficulties, the schools seem to fall down. Well let me explain.

One Sunday Pearl tried four times to telephone you, her Daddy that is, at your office in Lagos to tell you she was so unhappy in the boarding house she wanted to leave. I said to her, "Pearly Dear what will your Daddy be able to do all those miles away when he hears you crying into the 'phone like that? Dry your eyes," I said. "Don't cry there's a good girl and Donald will drive you back up to school straight to sick bay and you tell Matron you've got this nasty cold in the head and no one will guess you've been crying and tomorrow after you've had a good sleep you'll see the world all different spread out before you, and your exam will be as easy as anything."

So, when she had gone with her case and the Doll (that's the nickname we use for Donald) I had the kitchen to myself and I telephoned the headmaster.

"Dr Huddlebug," I said. "Pardon me if I've got your name wrong." It's a new man there I expect you know him. I've never met him. "Dr Huddlebug, I'm sorry to trouble you but it's about Pearl Page (Class 5E housemistress Mrs Kay) she's in love with my son Donald and she wants to leave school. As you will know she comes out here for all her free weekends and I've been trying to persuade her to stop on at school to finish the year out and get her leaving certificate. She's a bit hysterical," I said. "That's all it is."

"Mrs Morgan," he said to me ever so cold. "Pearl Page does not stand a chance of getting her leaving certificate. So far as the School is concerned she can leave tomorrow."

There was nothing I could say to that and I thought of you paying out all those fees for boarding school for eight years and then him to be so offhand just when she needed help. To cut things short. Pearl left school and came to stay with us, you know all this from her letters. I was a bit surprised you never wrote to me even when I wrote to you as of course it's been a big responsibility for me and even more for Donald who is not really old enough for a responsibility like Pearl.

Now there's nothing at all to get worried about. Just don't you worry! You're a long way off and you have a very busy life with a lot of entertaining to do, and I can guess what it must be like having to be gay and bright slipping in business deals while pleasuring yourselves and other people when you've a lot to worry about. It's hard enough looking after jarrah seedlings and poultry if you've lost your peace of mind. But I feel I must explain the situation you see it's got quite beyond me and I'm not sure if what I'm doing is right for all concerned. You may be quite certain I didn't rush into anything and I thought it all out very carefully first.

Pearl is very well. Indeed everyone who sees her remarks on it. She really glows with health and she eats very well. Growing our own vegetables we have everything very nice and fresh and there's always plenty. She seems happy in the nursing school and she studies really hard. In her time off she sits with her notes and diagrams and is so interested I am sure she has done right to go in for nursing. When it is time for her to come off duty Doll goes over to the hospital to fetch her and when it is time for her to go back he takes her. It's quite a drive as we are a couple of miles up the valley from the turn off at the twenty nine mile peg. It doesn't matter to him what time it is eleven p.m. shift or the six forty five in the morning. In fact his whole life has changed to accommodate Pearl's duty and off duty times and this means he is not able to have a job himself. It is three months now that this state of affairs is going on and when I say, "Pearly Dear, if Donald has a job and was not here you could easily catch the train and come out couldn't you? It does not take so very much longer on the train and I could fetch you from the station."

And she says, "Oh yes Mrs Morgan," and smiles at me from the sofa where she has all her study books on a cushion on her lap and Doll is sprawled there beside her reading comics till it is time to turn on the television. I don't know if you can picture how I feel Mrs Page and Mr Page when I see my son who is almost twenty waiting for the four o'clock children's session on the television. All he seems able to do these days it to watch telly and wait for Pearl to have done with her studying. And I am out in my kitchen trying to concentrate on some vegetables to put with a shank end, and all I can think of is my son being so idle and useless and not interested in anything.

You see Mrs Page and Mr Page things have not been all that easy with Donald. He left school before he should have and I'll never know the reason because he doesn't ever give reasons. I don't think he knows how to put his reasons into words. All I know is he won't compromise himself and consequently he cuts off his own nose to spite his face. Repeatedly. After leaving school he worked hard though he kept on changing jobs sometimes not staying long enough in one place to get his first pay even. In his own way I suppose he is protesting. I often wonder if he would have been better if his granny had come when we left our own country and I do wonder too what he would have been like if we had of all stayed back over there. Who can tell? I'll never know and I'll never know what he's protesting about. He always used to work hard feeding the fowls here for me and fixing things about the house and the sheds. Sometimes when he came from work I met him on the back verandah with the hammer and the screwdriver and he never minded. And when he was out of a job he'd paint a room or a ceiling or go in for something, little pine trees it was once. He potted a hundred pines one night before tea. He was in a real frenzy to get it done while it was still light.

"In thirty years mom," he said to me, "we'll all be rich." As it turned out the land just here where we are is not suited to pine trees. But I digress.

The fact is that I can't bear to see him the way he is now doing nothing. While Pearl is plump and pink Donald is grey and thin and haggard and his face is so set he looks like an old man. And when I try to talk to him he thinks I am interfering and he just snarls at me.

Pearl came to us first as Mary's friend. It is quite usual for day pupils to invite boarders and when Mary, who was still at school then, said,

"You know Peril Page at my school well she wants to come to stay, can I ask her?"

"You mean Pearl Page?" I said really pleased that our shy Mary had suggested bringing someone home from her class. I had to get dressed up a bit and go over to school to make the arrangement. They don't let the boarders go just anywhere of course.

"Pearl Page is a very *fine* girl Mrs Morgan," Mrs Kay said, she seems to have been housemistress there since kingdom come.

"Oh we will take great care of Pearl while she is with us," I hastened to assure Mrs Kay, to set her mind easy. I couldn't help wondering though what harm that woman was afraid could come to Pearl at our place. To put it in a nutshell Pearl hadn't been in the house ten minutes but she had the Doll's jersey on and, after that, she hadn't a look or a word for Mary who, after she'd cried her eyes out, tried to make the best of it.

A bit later we left our street and came to live in this valley under an agreement made with the gentleman who bought it when our grandpa died. One day Doll said he wanted to have Pearl Page for the weekend.

"You mean Peril Page from my school?" Mary asked. She had left by this time.

"Correct," the Doll said.

"Well of course!" I said, very surprised as Doll has never ever wanted to have anyone to stay and of course you know the rest and you will know too that we have always done everything we could to make her a welcome guest in our house. And you know how things have turned out up to the present time. I kept hoping you would be coming to your place in Greatmount. Pearl says you have a lovely home just out from town and will be coming back one day. If you were there now all this would never have happened the way it has. Still, that's neither here nor there is it?

Though I really love Pearl I don't forget how she dumped Mary and it is remembering this makes me afraid that when she has had all she wants from Donald she will look for better prospects and leave him for a fourth year medical student. (4th year is when they get out on to the wards and meet all the nurses.) This wouldn't matter so much if Donald was making his own way in life. But he isn't. His life at present is all Pearl and I don't know how it will ever end and this is why I have done what I have done and I can only hope it will be for the best.

As I said I made Pearl welcome as a guest and I'm not saying she doesn't appreciate it, she does, and that's what makes it all the harder.

First I gave Pearl Donald's bed and I put him on the couch in the kitchen then later it seemed better for Pearl to have Mary's little room and Mary moved in with me. The inconvenience caused by giving Pearl Mary's room is a bit stupid really as she is always in Donald's room. All her clothes and jars and bottles and things are in there too. But you do see don't you how I have to make it look as if I expect her to have a room to herself because of Mary who I am trying to bring up properly? And of course the people from down our street where we used to live visit us sometimes and customers come for eggs and people are so quick to see things and talk about them aren't they?

I know we have to move with the times, values are different now. These days young people have more freedom because of the pill but I don't know how to fit this freedom in with the way I am supposed to provide a background of good example and moral standards for my own girl. Let's face it if Mary went wrong people would say at once "Well look at the kind of house her mother keeps". I can't help wondering what other mothers do. What do you think about it Mrs Page?

It is because of all this I spoke to Pearl and Donald today.

"Pearl and Donald," I said. They were just making poached eggs for themselves when I came in at four o'clock pretty tired as a lady had stopped by and ordered a dozen dressed ducks and wanted them done straight away. "Pearl and Donald," I said. "After the end of this month which is in a week's time I am sorry to be the one to have to say that if young Doll here does not have a job by then you Pearl will have to stay in the hospital for your time off. You have a lovely room there Pearl Dear and the other nurses are all very nice girls and you will have to stop with them," I said. "Things can't go on as they are. I can't go on encouraging this situation and I'm sure you will agree with me, Pearly Dear, if we both really love Donald we want to see him out working getting on and earning his living and being with people. So Donald," I said, "So young Doll, no job, no Pearl to stop with us."

And Pearl smiled at me.

"Oh yes Mrs Morgan," and she dished out the eggs. I was shaking inside because I thought Donald would go for me and make a scene.

"I really mean this Donald," I said as firmly as I could. "One week from today. You have till the end of this one week."

And he just said,

"Yes Mom," ever so gently. Just like that, "Yes Mom."

I feel really terrible about what I've done Mrs Page and Mr Page. It is in my nature to love and cherish these two children and what I've done really hurts me. I feel I can't bear to go through with it but I'll have to. I've got to do something. And as well as this I can't help wondering whatever is going to happen at the end of this week.

# Night Report

---

---

December 1st Night Sister's Report.
<u>Room 3</u>  Mother voided 4 a.m. Nothing abnormal to report.
                                        signed Night Sister M. Shady.
December 2nd Night Sister's Report
<u>Room 3</u>  Mother and Mrs Hailey voided 4 a.m. Nothing abnormal to
report.                          Signed Night Sister M. Shady.
December 3rd Night Sister's Report
<u>Room 3</u>  Mother voided also Mrs Hailey and Mrs Renfrew. Nothing
abnormal to report.              Signed Night Sister M. Shady.
*<u>Night Sister Shady:</u>  Please will you report more fully.  Please report*
*on the other patients.  You are supposed to wash the kitchen floor*
*too you seem to have forgotten this.  I seem to have to remind you*
*too often that if a patient upsets her tea in bed you are to boil up*
*some water and pour on at once.  All my sheets are getting ruined.*
*Also my brother Lt. Col. (retired) Shroud has something to add.*
*signed Matron A. Shroud.*

*"TO ALL NIGHT STAFF TO WHOM IT MAY CONCERN IT HAS*
*COME TO MY NOTICE THAT STAFF ARE USING THE TELEPHONE*
*FOR THEIR PERSONAL LIFE THIS MUST CEASE IMMEDIATELY"*
*signed I. Shroud (Lt. Col. Retired).*

December 4th Night Sister's Report
<u>Room 3</u>  Mother voided room three sponged slept well 4 a.m. Kitchen
floor washed as request.  Sweet potatoes prepared also pumpkin
please matron can I have a knife for the vegetables. Nothing abnormal
to report.                          signed Night Sister M. Shady.
*<u>Night Sister Shady:</u>  It is unfortunate that one of the patients is your*

*mother please will you refer to her in this report book as Mrs Morgan which is her correct name. Please bring your own knife it is simply not practical for me to provide knives as all previous night nurses have left and taken them away. Please report more fully and why always 4 a.m.? Is this the only time you know? Please boil beetroots.*

*Signed Matron A. Shroud.*

December 5th Night Sister's Report

Room 3 It's about mother I mean Mrs Morgan Matron. At 4 a.m. all patients voided and had terrible words. Sweet potatoes have gone mouldy. Beetroots boiled as requested. N.A. to report.

signed Night Sister M. Shady.

*Night Sister Shady: Please report more fully. What about the patients in rooms 1 and 2 and please explain why always 4 a.m. Surely things happen at other times in the night. And what do you mean "Nothing abnormal to report"? Mrs Morgan's sheets were all covered in blood this morning and why is her foot bandaged? You seem to have forgotten the kitchen floor, this is to be done every night. Mrs Thompson says she has not had a bath since you took over night duty. And please clean thoroughly the saucepan you ruined last night. Mrs Thompson's bath should be at 10 p.m. Please write a detailed account of what happened last night. Write on a clean page in this book.*

*Signed Matron A. Shroud.*

December 6th Night Sister's Report but first the Detailed Account. First I am sorry Matron about the time 4 a.m. There is no clock here as you know and so when the milk comes I know it is four o'clock as he is punctual and I hear his Word when he falls on the broken step out there.

About Mrs Morgan's foot matron. Ever since you moved mother in with those other patients they've gone for each other and at 4 a.m. she got really wild with Mrs Hailey and Mrs Renfrew and she slipped and caught her foot in the bedside commode and the nail came off. Wound dressed p.r.n. with menthol camphor. I could not change her bed as I used the clean sheet matron for Mrs Hailey's bed after mother tipped the flowers all over. I am sorry matron about rooms 1 and 2, I did not realise there were patients there.

And about the saucepan it could not be helped the beetroots caught while I was so busy in room 3.

Night Sister's Report following Detailed Account

Saucepan cleaned as well as could be expected. Prepared bath for Mrs Thompson 10 p.m.

Mrs Thompson came in 4 a.m. She said she never asked for a bath and anyway the water was cold by then. Mrs Thompson and these two elderly gentlemen was very noisy they said they wanted sandwiches but I explained to them the 'fridge was locked and showed them your padlock. What about a drink then they said and Mrs Thompson showed us where you keep the Hospital Brandy Matron they all had a medicinal dose I hope this is satisfactory. Slept well.

Dressed Mother's wound again p.r.n. with menthol camphor, Matron I really think I need some help in room 3.

signed Night Sister M. Shady.

*Night Sister Shady: No it is not satisfactory the brandy is for my own personal use. Please remember this. Patients are to bring in their own brandy if required. Kindly note your mother's name for the purposes of this book is Mrs Morgan. Why did you use menthol camphor? And again the kitchen floor was not washed and the saucepan will not do.*

*Signed Matron A. Shroud.*

December 7th Night Sister's Report

Menthol camphor is the only ointment I can find. Bath prepared for Mrs Thompson as requested. Patient did not come in till 4 a.m. also Mr Doll and Mr Fingers. They said they had eaten and only needed the medicinal dose. In going along the passage they disturb room 3 who was only just got off to sleep so I sponge all 4 a.m. Nothing abnormal to report.

signed Night Sister M. Shady

*Night Sister Shady   Who is this Mr Doll and what is his diagnosis? And Mr Fingers ditto. There is no one of those names in this hospital. Please look on the list on the back of the bathroom door and see for yourself. Again you say "Nothing abnormal to report" but what was all my linen doing in the passage and why was the door wrenched off the sideboard also the padlock on the refrigerator has been forced and why have all the contents of the cupboards in room 3 been put on Mrs Morgan's bed she is quite unable to get into it. Please remember she is 98. Menthol camphor is not the only remedy we have. On the shelf under the sink is a tin of Epsom Salts. In an emergency why don't you use your eyes. Mrs Thompson complains that it seems too much trouble for you to prepare the bath and she did not like to have it because of this. Please remember to boil the beetroots or they will go off and I need them for the cold trays on Sunday. And Night Sister Shady, <u>Kitchen Floor</u>.*

*Signed Matron A. Shroud.*

*My brother I. Shroud Lt. Col. (Retired) has prepared 2 notices pin them up please.*

---

*TO ALL NIGHT STAFF TO WHOM IT MAY CONCERN IT HAS COME TO MY NOTICE THAT STAFF ARE USING THE TELEPHONE FOR THEIR PERSONAL LIFE THIS MUST CEASE IMMEDIATELY.*
*Signed I. M. Shroud Lt. Col. Retired .*

---

---

*IT HAS COME TO MY NOTICE THAT ALL JUNKETS ARE DAILY.*
*Signed I M Shroud Lt. Col. (Retired).*

---

December 8th Night Sister's Report

Beetroots boil as request also bath for Mrs Thompson 10 p.m. Patient came in quite early also Mr Doll and Mr Fingers when I ask her about the bath she says she never took one and Mr Doll says Betsy Thompson never in her life took anything bigger than a silver tea pot and they roar their heads off laughing they make so much noise they wake room 3 and there is another picnic here like last night and they play this game matron where all hunt for the bottle of medicinal. That is why all that confusion last night. I did not have time to clear up. Really matron I think I need some help at night. Mr Doll says he wants to be a patient too if you will have him please also Mr Fingers, he is Mr Shady I am sorry matron we are related Mr Doll is also called Mr Morgan so he is a relation too. I am sorry.

Mr Fingers Shady medicinal dose taken 4 a.m. Slept well

Mr Doll Morgan medicinal dose 4 a.m. Slept well

Mrs Thompson medicinal dose 4 a.m. Slept well

Room 3 medicinal dose 4 a.m. voided. Slept well.

Nothing abnormal to report.
Signed Night Sister M Shady

*Night Sister Shady: Who wants to read about junkets in the bathroom. In future please use your head for notices. Kitchen floor please and will you clean burned saucepan.*
*signed Matron A. Shroud.*

December 9th Night Sister's Report. Very sorry about notices Matron but bathroom door is the only one soft enough to take a drawing pin. 10 p.m.  Bath prepared for Mrs Thompson also kitchen floor and saucepan.  Patient came in early and asked to have a water fight Mr D Morgan and Mr Fingertips did not come and as patient seemed distressed I said well just a very little water fight then.

Report on condition of equipment 1. Taps 2. Curtains 3. Requisition.
1 The shower tap broke off it is only banged on with my shoe matron so be careful please or else you loose all your water.

2  The shower curtain will need fixing there is a weakness in the bathroom wall near the shower curtain.  And 3 please could we have another pane of glass in the bathroom window (3 is Requisition). Doll and Fingertips came in 4 a.m.  They said they wanted to be sure Betsy had settled. All comfortable slept well.

Room 3  Very quiet all night. Nothing abnormal to report.

Signed Night Sister M Shady

*Night Sister Shady  Please remember, for the purposes of this report book Mrs Thompson is not Betsy but Mrs B Thompson.  Of course Room 3 was very quiet all night Mrs Morgan and the other patients were moved to the City and District Hospital to have their injuries treated.  Don't you ever read my Day Report?*

*My brother I. M. Shroud (Lt. Col. Retired) will be sleeping in room 3 for the present. Please give him hot milk 10 p.m. also Mrs Thompson's bath and kitchen floor.*

*And Night Sister Shady it has come to my notice that you are unregistered please note that your pay will be adjusted as from when you took up duties in this hospital.  I shall be obliged to address you as Mrs Shady but for the Good Name of this Hospital you will continue as Night Sister M. Shady (unregistered).*

*Signed Matron A. Shroud.*

December 10th  Night Sister's Report (unregistered)
Room 3  Hot milk prepared for Lt Col I M Shroud 10 p.m.  Lt Col says why on earth Amy because he never touches the stuff. Patient very restless and distressed.

Mother came in 4 a.m. also Mrs Hailey and Mrs Renfrew discharged from the City and District Hospital.  Satisfactory.  Mrs Thompson came in 4 a.m. also Doll and Fingertips the milkman fell and bruise himself very awkward place dressed with menthol camphor 4 a.m. All play cards in the dinette Lt Col Shroud brighten up but loose badly.

Nothing abnormal to report.

signed Night Sister M. Shady (unregistered).

*Mrs M Shady:  Please note no christian names on duty I refer of*
*course to my brother's use of mine.  What do you mean nothing*
*abnormal to report.  I never heard of patients being discharged from*
*the City and District Hospital at 4 a.m.  And please remember the*
*milkman is not a patient here.  What about the kitchen floor what do*
*you do all night?*

Signed Matron A. Shroud.
*(please note spelling of lose)*

December 11th Night Sister's Report

Hot milk and bath prepared 10 p.m.  Mrs Thompson came in early
also Doll and Fingertips.  What about a game of cards they wanted to
know so all play cards in the dinette.  They all play this game Matron
it's all raise a dollar kings on queens raise two dollars 3 bullets raise
three dollars it's a real scream it's a picnic matron I don't think I ever
saw Mother enjoy herself so well. Lt. Col. Shroud really enjoying
himself but lose badly. N.A. to report.

signed Night Sister M. Shady.

*Mrs Shady  You realise of course two packs should be used one pack*
*for playing while the other is shuffled.  Please see that this is done.*
*signed Matron A. Shroud.*

December 12th  Night Sister's Report  your instructions noted.  All
patients in early all play cards in dinette. Lt. Col. Shroud lose very
badly.  Nothing abnormal to report.

Signed Night Sister M. Shady.

*Mrs Shady: Your report noted.*

*signed Matron A. Shroud.*

December 13th Night Sister's Report

Patients all in early all play cards in dinette. Lt. Col. Shroud enjoying
himself but lose all the time. N.A. to report.

Signed Night Sister M. Shady.

*Mrs Shady: Your report noted.*

*signed Matron A. Shroud.*

December 14th Night Sister's Report

All pats. in early all play cards in dinette. Lt. Col. Shroud lose.
Request from Lt. Col. Shroud he says Amy can he have his pocket
money early also if you sell up what is his share?

signed Night Sister M. Shady

December 15th Night Sister's Report

Cards in dinette. All pats. satisfactory. Lt. Col. lose very heavy.
Request from Lt. Col. repeated he says I would like to know Amy
how soon you can sell up and what my share is. N.A. to report.

signed Night Sister M. Shady.

### December 16th Night Sister's Report

Cards. Lt. Col. lose. Request repeated. also Doll and Fingertips say
cough up or else and Mother says even if hospital is no longer
yours you can still be matron as we shall need one. Nothing
abnormal to report.

signed Night Sister M. Shady

### December 17th Night Sister's Report.

Cards in dinette. Satisfactory Lt. Col. Shroud lose. N.A. to report.

Signed Night Sister M. Shady

*Mrs Shady: In future I shall be taking your place on Night Duty.
Please leave uniform overall on nail on back of bathroom door also
cards where I can find them. There will naturally be a vacancy now on
the day shift. If you are interested will you please report at 7 a.m.
and start by washing the Kitchen floor which has not been done for
some time also boil beetroots for the cold trays on Sunday. You will
of course write the Day Report on the appropriate pages in this book.*

*signed Matron A. Shroud.*

### December 19th Day Sister's Report.

Very quiet day. Pats. play cards in dinette. Lt. Col. lose badly. Nothing abnormal to report.

Signed Day Sister M. Shady

## Poppy Seed and Sesame Rings


Tante Bertl collapsed and died without my being able to do anything about it on the steps of the Art Gallery and Museum. It was on the way home from a short afternoon visit to Grossmutti.

We sat, all three together, in the watery green light of her small apartment, the room opened into a conservatory and the winter sun, fading, made a delicate pattern of fern shadows on the coffee coloured lace table cloth. Tante Bertl sighed repeatedly.

"Das schmeckt mir," she said, taking a third cream filled pastry. "Wirklich gut!" Tante Bertl's voice was contented.

"Only try and walk," I implored her, pulling at her plump hand. It was such a public place though, at the time, no one was walking there or sitting on the benches. She had insisted on getting off at the Museum. A light rain was falling.

"Let us make a little rain walk," she said and, clambering on her short fat legs from the tram, she sank down on to the bottom step of that wide flight which seemed to reach up behind her to the sky.

As if I were the cause of her difficulties I felt ashamed and embarassed. I glanced round quickly and nervously, anyone could see us there, even the pigeons could notice us in our trouble. I was afraid she was going to be sick there on the pavement.

I tried to pull her from the step but she only sighed and, making no attempt to get up, she simply leaned forward and died. I ran straight home leaving her there with the pigeons and the coming darkness.

"Tante Bertl wanted to walk," I told them so they did not expect her for a time.

I thought I heard Mother crying in the night, her subdued sighs followed my father creaking on bent legs about the shop. I knew Tante Bertl was dead. All night long I pictured her huddled all alone on the steps of the Museum with its strange and grotesque treasures piled up behind her. Would the pigeons come to her I wondered, or would they avoid a dead old lady smelling of the vague warm sweetness of old age and so stuffed with pastries.

"Go to sleep, it's all right, go to sleep," in the candle light my father crawled flickering across the ceiling crouching doubled on the cupboard, "it's nothing, it's all right, everything's all right, go to sleep." Flickering and prancing he moved up and down the walls big and little and big and I heard Mother crying and crying.

Next day Mother had to go to the mortuary. My father said to me, "You go with her and comfort her." I did not want to go but my father could not leave the shop he said, and I knew this was so. Mother felt so strange in the New Country and she tried to make friends with the few customers we had. She was always giving away packets of groceries or bars of chocolate and washing soap.

"Take ziss too, but take ziss, " she said, trying to imitate the tone and the accent of the people who were now her neighbours. She wanted to be accepted by these people and she pushed the presents my father could not afford to give into the spaces in their shopping baskets.

There were not many corpses in the mortuary. Tante Bertl's body looked so small as if it had been cut in half. I wondered if there would be a mess of blood and pastry, a body cut in half would be a terrible sight unless there was some clever method that I didn't know about. While Mother was being led away towards the white enamelled door, I hurriedly lifted the bottom end of the cloth.

Tante Bertl's unexpected feet gave me a shock. I had never seen her bare feet before, they were plump and neat and very clean. They were wide apart. I supposed this was because of her fat thighs.

It seemed then, that a person was very small in death.

At once Grossmutti came to stay. With her tin trunk and wicker-work baskets, she sat in the back room and disapproved of Mother's marriage to a shopkeeper. When Grossmutti came she usually stayed for several weeks her disapproval mounting daily until, after a series of small explosions, she entered into a grand packing and a departure, after which things went on as before. Except that this time there would be no Tante Bertl to nudge Mother softly and whisper with her in the back room.

Mother wept aloud and wished for Bertl.

"Recha!" said Grossmutti. "Stop sniffing and get my bed made up in the spare room and send Louise up with some hot coals, the room's sure to be damp."

The night was long and I heard my father creaking to and fro over the floorboards.

"Who's that!" Grossmutti's voice crackled in the darkness, she always kept her door open keeping an unasked for vigil over her son-in-law and his house.

"It is only me," he replied softly. "I am looking for fly spray. Mosquito."

"No mosquito this time of year. More likely vermin!" And then she called, "What for is Recha crying?"

"It is all right," my father patiently explained. "She is home-sick that is all." Grossmutti made a sound of scorn and disbelief.

I often heard Mother crying in the night. When I called out my father always explained in a soft voice, "She is homesick, that is all." So I always knew what was the matter. Sometimes, after those times, Mother sent me out for fillet of veal cut in thin slices, she hammered the meat on the red tiles of the kitchen floor and sang,

"Mein' Schätzlein ist sauber ist weiss wie die Schnee – "

And after dinner, when the shop was closed, my father got up from the table, slapped his thighs and leapt across the room, and Mother, with a demure expression, danced sedately round and round the dinner table with him.

My poor mother was always homesick. She longed for the scenery and the smells and for the people of her homeland. She blamed her marriage for all that she was suffering.

"Why are you crying so?" my father, perplexed, would ask her. "We have a nice house and a shop and a good life safe here in the New Country. What you wanted isn't it? You and your sister and your mother. Really it is as if I have married all three of you to bring you here, all safe, and you are not satisfied," he scratched his fine sandy hair. "And," he said, "And I bring Louise too because you are used to her even though she will soon be too old to work," his voice climbed in indignation. "Really it is as if I marry four women to bring out," he said. He looked at me, "But five," he said and shrugged helplessly.

Mother longed for the bread she had been used to all her life at home. Though we had poppy seed bread and sesame rings, she said they were not the same at all. Often she took a small roll from the glass sided cupboard where the bread was kept and she broke the bread and sniffed it and dipped it in her coffee.

"It is not the same," she moaned softly.

I too liked to break the fresh bread and sniff it and pile it into my coffee and pick up the succulent fragrant lumps with a spoon. But with Mutti in the back room we had to refrain from these habits only fit for shopkeepers.

At school I learned the alimentary system of the rabbit. I knew the rabbit from the pinna to the tail. I learned all the latin names of the human skeleton by heart and all the details of internal combustion and gaseous interchange. I sorted out in my mind the mingling and exchanging of the various juices involved in the process of digestion. And when we had examinations I was always top of the class.

Because of old age, Louise had to leave us and then Grossmutti died. No catastrophe, she just fell asleep quietly like a doll in the little bedroom.

And the years went by one after the other.

"Your mother has no one," my father said to me in his soft concerned voice. He was so busy in the shop, his skin was paler than ever from being indoors all the time. He never went anywhere and the shop did not change. It did not prosper and it did not give up. The same foods were there and the same customers starting at half past seven in the morning wanting small purchases until nine o'clock at night. The shop was only closed on Good Friday and on Christmas Day. Our own holidays and feasts were pushed aside left in a bygone life. I had been too young when we left to remember this other life but Mother continued to weep alone in the dingy room at the back.

"She is alone all the time. You might try and come and see her more often," my father said at the end of one of my rare visits. He was in the closed shop with me, the smell of mixed delicatessen and spices seemed sharper because of the dark. I had to be back at the hospital for the night.

"I'm pretty busy these days," I made the excuse.

"Yes yes but your mother is always waiting for you to come," he made a movement of self effacing apology with his hands in which, even his shoulders and neck and head, even his whole body, took part.

"Your father is working all the time," Mother reproached me during the short visit. "He has never a holiday, always working and working so that you can study and pass your exam."

She always spoke as if I had only one examination to pass. My whole life had become a series of tests and examinations and the only friends I had were books and scalpels and test tubes and dry dead bones. My father toiled so that I could study so that is what I did.

I promised my father I would come home more often and I ran like a thief, with nothing stolen except some hours from my studying, through the empty streets all the way to the hospital.

I resolved to find a friend and to take her home with me the very next week to end my loneliness and to please Mother.

Of course it took longer than I expected and I did not go home for a whole month.

"Go in to her!" my father was just closing the shutters. "Every day she waits and waits hoping you will come." She was sitting in the back behind the shop, that was all she had to do, just sit. There was scarcely enough work for two people in the shop.

I explained quickly I was coming on Sunday.

"I'm bringing Marion," I said trying to make it sound like a treat.

"Who is Marion?" Mother asked. "Who is this Marion?"

"She is my friend from the hospital," I explained nervously.

"Does she study too for exam?" Mother asked.

"She works in the hospital," I said.

"How can she work there and not study?" Mother wanted to know.

"There is other work," I said, "all kinds of work."

"Sunday, you close the shop," Mother said to my father, "we have a visitor coming." She seemed pleased. "Sunday afternoon, we close the shop," she said.

"So!" my father said. "Good! good!" he rubbed his pale soft hands together. I hoped Marion would be a success, but at the back of my mind were some grave doubts.

As soon as we arrived Mother made it very clear that she had not rested, that she had worked without stopping for some days. The table was covered with dishes, bean salad, herring salad, potato salad, even cabbage salad, the air was heavy with their various dressings. There was a large flat plate of cold meat, veal coated with sauce, liver sausage and salami slices and hard boiled eggs, enough for a dozen people. There were cakes too, pastries filled with jam and cream and little heart shaped biscuits.

"She has not made these things for years," my father said happily. But he had not yet noticed Mother's face as I brought in Marion. I hardly knew my new friend. I had chosen her because she looked healthy and very clean and was the nearest one to speak to at the counter in the hospital administration department. She had seemed pleased to be invited to my home on Sunday. She was a big girl, bigger than all of us, I had not noticed this before. Her pink blouse filled our living room. She kept talking too, from the minute we entered, trying to be well behaved and say the right things. Mother's face was dark with disapproval and it became worse especially as Marion couldn't pronounce our name. She kept calling Mother Mrs. Mosh.

"I love the embroidered cushions Mrs. Mosh, did you make them?" and "That's a dream of a dress you have on Mrs. Mosh."

"Nothing but personal remark!" Mother snapped at me in the scullery.

"She is only trying to be friends," I whispered uneasily.

"She is not any friend for you, she is not ours!" she said so vehemently, I knew she could never receive anyone for me from this New Country as she still thought of it. Just then the radio came on. Mother flew into the living room.

"In this house I switch on or off the wireless!" she said grimly. Years of unhappiness had made her like this I knew but I wished she would try to be agreeable.

Marion blushed.

"It's a lovely radio," she said. "Pardon me! but I just love music. Do you like classical music Mrs. Mosh?" There was a silence after Mother had switched off, Marion hummed quietly.

"Tell your friend she is not Beethoven," Mother said coldly. And then she helped Marion to a big plateful of meats and salads even though Marion protested,

"Oh no more thank you Mrs. Mosh! If I eat all that I'll be like the side of a house!" She was buried in egg and salami.

In his embarrassment my father stood up and passed plates to Marion all in the wrong order.

"Cake?" he said in his gentle voice. "Biscuit? All home-made!" I wanted to ask him to wait. I felt it was all my fault this terrible afternoon.

"Oh very nice I'm sure," Marion thanked him, "But I'll have to refuse. I'll be putting on pounds. I've got a spare tyre already!"

"Look such waste!" Mother snatched Marion's plate from me angrily in the scullery. "You see she does not like our food even!" she scraped the plate noisily into the pail under the sink.

I felt I couldn't face the impossible evening which lay ahead but Marion solved this.

"Well," she said smiling all round the table, after the meal. "I'll just have to be going now. I have enjoyed myself really I have Mrs. Mosh. Thank you so very much Mrs. Mosh for having me and thank you Mr. Mosh."

My father, who was already on his feet, gave a little bow which seemed to involve his whole body, and I jumped up gratefully.

"I'll go with you," I said, and I fetched our rain coats. At the bus stop Marion said there was no need to go all the way with her, she would be all right, she said. She waved to me from inside the bus and, from the wet pavement, I waved to her.

I thought I ought to go back home.

I ran straight back and Mother was quite different. There was a smell of fresh coffee and she had put some stale poppy seed rolls and a sesame ring from the shop into the oven. All her photograph albums were on the table. Not a word was said about Marion. It was as if she had never been there. We spent the evening in another world with Tante Bertl, Grossmutti and Louise and myself when I was a child. At intervals my father exclaimed in his gentle voice,

"Ach so! Look at this one!" and, "this is a good picture, take a look at your mother in this picture she has not changed has she." It was just as if we were looking at the photographs for the first time. Mother talked and laughed and recalled the materials and the colours of our dresses, and the various occasions. One happy time after another, she described them all.

Then she busily packed up some cold meats and pastries and I had to run all the way to catch the last bus to the hospital. The hard boiled eggs were coming through the wet paper, so I left the parcel in a deserted waiting room on the ground floor.

Upstairs I sat at my table and tried to read and write and study but I kept writing Marion's name everywhere.

I thought about her. I kept thinking about her without being able to do anything about it.

Because of her it seemed that the diagram of the systemic circulation was all wrong. Suddenly it was clear to me that blood flowed in all directions at once. The twelve pairs of cranial nerves, I knew them all by heart, were said to govern the special senses but now I knew these special senses had no government. I thought I would write about the lymphatic system, but instead I began to write about quiet lakes and deep pools which have no reflection and no memory; I wrote too about the excitement of the secluded places where land and water meet.

In my thoughts I found I had an unknown store-house of feelings and I wrote them into half remembered sunsets and half known ways leading through secret woods and along hidden river banks. As I wrote during the night of these strange and grotesque treasures it seemed as if the fragrance of fresh grass came from somewhere not far beyond the hospital and the roof tops and the chimneys. Somewhere in the world I knew there were mountains and more mountains. I wanted a whole mountain to myself. In the night I wanted to be on the mountain climbing up to reach the clear air and the magic place on the peak just when the first sunlight would reach it too.

In the morning I wrote Marion's name again and again on every piece of paper on my study table. And in my hand my pen had an innocence I did not quite understand.

# ANIA WALWICZ

## Picture

To have children. She said. If you did. That would calm down. You.
What. We'll bring it up. If you don't want it. I thought I was pregnant. Shingles. You are a nervous girl. My mother. Has children.
You got to. She said. I wanted to. I loved you. She. Mother. Woman.
Children. That she was sick with me. That she was sick while she
was waiting for me. That it was hard. So hard. She said. Have children. Wait. Then you'll know what it's like. I don't want them. You
can't spend your life. Alone. No. You just can't. Have man. A. Doesn't
matter. If it isn't mister right. The black stick figure. Ania lives with
a man. Good. We're not going to criticise. Mister stick figure. The
stick man. Big stick man. He stands in front. My body. Turns to clay.
I am in a hot desert. My hair turns black. From worry. Why don't
you. Have a baby. My mother said. He said. If baby. Then marry.
Woman. Earth. Mother. Terry. In a desert. Waiting for her baby. To
come. Baby. Mother. Expecting. Put a halo round. Her head. She's in
blessed state. Give your seat to her bus. She is pregnant. My mother.
Baby. Photograph. Always angry. Mother goddess. Gold. Outlined.
She is wife. Mrs. Marry. She got somebody. Baby. It was important to
be like that. She said. Don't worry. Have a baby. The stick figure
huddles inside me. Have the baby she said. We will bring it up. My
mother with baby. Always angry. She follows. The picture. Virgin
Mary. With baby. This made her important. She told me. She made
me.

*Ania Walwicz*

## Doorstop

snake sneaky what he got between my legs nothing not that hasn't
grown my father has one i saw they have these snakes between i
want to pee like that i try and i try and nothing happens it runs
down my leg she told me you can't now you're a girl i was watching
how the stream and how curved how he stood how it goes like a
jet i always wanted one too yes please why not as well looking little
boys my father wanted me too have boy short hair in trousers i look
my best he says i look little boys me too henio he calls me henio
henio henio is a boys' what is can i have one too i don't know
what happened that i'd like it better to stand the jet to have one my
father wants a boy he didn't want me no girl little no take this pretty
dress off immediately it doesn't suit you at all i snake to have trousers
to have a boy my father takes me to the barber's i have my hair cut
as short as short hair cut razor up my neck close shave ask the barber
do you want vaseline in your hair my father wants boys i want to
please i can be a boy oh yes be a boy call me henio he calls me henio
i boy little henio always in trousers art books in his room going for
walks i hold his hand he loves me little boy i'll be boy little for you
i am a boy i am good at school i'm going to be famous lawyer
professor something great i never wear ribbons not silly do you study
enough my father gives me my snake give me my snake he gave me
that special the king he rides with me at night in bed together me and
my father he holds my hand because i was seeing alligators tell me
poems the earl king rides at night he gave me this boy ride night be a
famous famous henio me henio now famous i get a snake me famous
henio famous without any dresses me fearless henio fearless fear not i
boy now henio my hair short hair i put the snake in my hand me
henio angry henio i can do anything yes i can i henio famous famous
snake in my hand if i can't have one i grab one i buy me one i have one
one have one snake one doorstop i am little angry henio boy not afraid
of the dark my father took it he cut it my vet dad castrating horses
why did you do me henio boy little father push enema up me made
me feel like that me henio boy little hair short short hands grown big
i am not myself and better that i was i'm feeling pretty good now
me henio boy angry little little boy now i am a boy i swing my snake
i henio boy little sick of keeping house i angry boy now don't want to
be your wife my father made me me henio boy little my father teach

me me little man don't want to look after roger me angry angry henio
little boy i swing my snake around my father gave me i boy in boy
my father did me henio now grown big man me i man now i've got a
snake in my hand doorstop to hit with i've got a snake in my hand
my tool draught stop doorstop snake to hit with i little boy henio
not wanting to keep house  sweet little thing sweetie don't want to
be like that i angry henio i hit him i hit him i hit him i angry henio
little killer grown to be a man i get him with my doorstop big make
fat sneaky in my hand i angry henio boy don't want to be your wife
i kill my father now

## Omen

all this before just the same that before just the same all happening before everything happens before this already before this happening before everything happened before so we know i know now that before already i had that yes the remember half way  down hill slid in the mud had that before already saw knew lived that have you had this have you felt that that that already done that yes that knew what next what strange this strange this i know what will happen next  yes i do i know i knew i will know some more in the future too i all know what in the park where fountain lived autumn bus go spa to a spa and dark too cold my stockings too thin cold snow spring like in between seasons that i had that where fountain where room where gold is where in a dream i always know what will happen next yes but i don't trust the i don't trust little house had that too cold to it don't come here look but i went in never should have gone said in the stars look out but i didn't listen i don't listen think first don't listen i had little house evil said don't but i went just the same the end of the forest walk park stood man next to a tree scare scare turn my bicycle ride away all before like it again and again i have the remember now voice says don't go there but i didn't listen should have listened should have never gone should have never gone should have listened and never went should have never ever went there should have never ever ever but i did

## Buttons

little i'm useful buttons little my tender buttons my button fell off
i didn't have a partner had to cut it off get two more buttons she cut
them off her coat she gave them to me these are old buttons don't
worry after i found another button sewn inside my jacket but it was too
late and i threw the other one out pink ones in a jar how many will
you have i'll have six or twelve yes twelve little with a shiny top i
want a button with a diamond on it fell off i'll stick it on i have
buttons with diamonds on top i wear them they keep my blouse
shut so i don't show off i have had button on a string around my
neck it was only one with little mirrors it was a grand big button on
my coat had huge buttons shiny buttons i had white buttons i
wanted black buttons i painted them black they were black buttons
made them had buttons on me sewn my mother told me put thread
between your teeth when i sew a button on your clothes you are
wearing so i don't sew you up so i don't sew your head so i won't
be stupid she sews buttons on me needle through eye attach to knot
and around and around tack it on so i stay on attached to my material
i don't lose a button i sew it on me firm my button is hard i had little
buttons on my cushions i have many buttons i play with my buttons
i play with my button i pushed a button up my nose i was little i
couldn't get it out pushed button up nose my what am i doing push
my button up my nose push it and push it and push push button up
nose i i don't know why i don't know why i am pushing this button
up my nose i didn't know i just have to do it i don't know why i do
it but i do i have to push a button up my nose i just had to do it
i had to push a button up my nose i had to i have to i have to do it
now they had to hold me by my legs till the button fell out that gave
me a scare i don't push maybe i won't push buttons up my nose now
maybe not i never push buttons up my nose now i promise i won't
do it i had to i had to i had to i just had to push the button i don't
know why but i do i don't know why i had to do it i don't know why
i had to push this button up my nose to push the button up my nose
but i did buttons wait for my finger button push button and i get
coffee and milk and sugar and cigarettes and comfortable i don't
have to do much i am easy button for me i put my finger little
buttons on a jumper tiny you are delightful i am tender i like you
little buttons she has a button i have a button too we have buttons

girls we girls have buttons to us we are sweet better than zips each button has a little hole for it to put my finger on a button buttons on her blouse one by one my button gets bigger i sew a button on i have a hard button every colour in you can buy buttons any size these are lovely i want this button for me yes please i sew my button i put thread in my mouth i learn buttons big silver you are elegant buttons on her dress pearly queens and kings buttons hard as bone smooth sewn around edges warm buttons on and buttons on sew my button on me i sew my button on me sew button on button on button me up unbutton me put your hand on the button buttons for my finger i am undone.

# ANDREA GOLDSMITH

## The Meal

**(Come Eat with Me and Be My Love and We Shall All the Pleasures Prove.)**

There is a man seated at a table in a restaurant. He appears to have lost something. What could it be? It cannot be his lover for he holds her hand in his own, rhythmically rubbing her knuckles with his thumb. He is looking down, at his plate. Something must be lost amid the empty oyster shells that form a circle on the metal dish. Has he lost an oyster? Is there one remaining, sunk into a crevice of a gnarled shell? But this is not possible. If he had been watching himself he would know that each single oyster had been eaten. Some minutes ago he took the little fork, and, with the precision of an accountant, poked his way around the circle of shells, clockwise, commencing at the 12 o'clock position. Fork to the edge of the shell, a stab and a twist, oyster to mouth, swallow. Oysters are rarely chewed. Their innards are not texturally consistent with their exterior. In fact, it is feasible that most people do not appreciate the gizzards of oysters. But oysters, being a social necessity, are nevertheless tolerated in a way that denies their interior. Slurp and swallow. The man has not disturbed the seafood sauce. It aggravates his chronic hay fever.

He has raised his eyes (diluted blue and too close together). He smiles briefly at his lover as his gaze passes hers on its pathway to a spot two thirds of the way up the wall to his right. Apart from paint there is nothing on this portion of wall. His thumb continues its pendulum motion across his lover's fingers. Back and forth. His caress has rubbed all sensation from the skin. His lover Evie looks at her enmeshed hand. He has erased her knuckles and is steadily penetrating the palm below. Her clammy palm. Has he noticed its wetness? It is doubtful he can register anything being so engrossed with the wall. Evie untangles her hand. Withdraws it. He jerks his head to the midline and sees her adjusting the position of her plate. She wipes her hand on her serviette. Was there food on the side of her plate, he wonders, did it touch her hand? He nods with approval and regains the hand when Evie returns it to its place on the table.

"Oysters good?" she asks.

"Mmm, very fresh. Yours?"

"Yes, lovely."

"Yes, you can tell when an oyster is fresh, can't you?"

"How?"asks Evie. A good manoeuvre she thinks, he loves answering questions.

"Well...Well, you know..."

"I don't think I do."

"Well, you'd certainly know a rotten oyster wouldn't you?" He is so patient.

"Yes, but is rotten to be equated with frozen?"

"Oh god Evie! You're so pedantic sometimes."

"Mmm, maybe you're right." Evie realises that oysters are a risky topic. Oysters will need to be added to that elastic list of 'topics to be avoided'. She wonders if she should include prawns, clams, mussels, scallops, lobster, crayfish and crab as well. 'AVOID TALK OF SHELLFISH' the item would say.

Evie and her lover continue to converse with remarks on the quality of the restaurant. They agree that the food here is very good, the service polite and efficient, and yes, they will recommend it to their friends. They blink at each other, they smile to each other. What do they see? Certainly they would like to see the waitress: this absence of structure is tedious.

They turn their heads expectantly. The waitress stands at one side of the table. The young couple disengage and sit back in their chairs. The waitress removes the plates. "Lovely," they say. She glances at them, nods, then disappears to the kitchen at the rear of the restaurant.

Now the man takes Evie's other hand. He fiddles with the ring on her third finger. He rocks it back and forth. With this mark of affection he hides the nail of the ring finger. Evie is relieved, the polish on this nail is chipped. She had no time to repair it due to the 'phonecall with her girlfriend earlier in the evening. Connie had rung at a most inopportune time but Evie had not wanted to be impolite. Besides, she likes Connie. Connie has problems. Connie does not have a boy-friend. This is not a problem to Connie; others regard it as a problem. They say that Connie will never be happy. No man could satisfy

Connie they say, she's too fussy and she's too smart. But Evie likes Connie and Connie likes Evie. They talk, they talk for hours. They talk about everything. Perhaps this explains why Evie has so little to say to her lover, the man who sits opposite her. If it were not for sex their silence would be intolerable. All that extra time and no words with which to absorb it. Sex does not require talking, so her lover believes. He does not speak when they are making love. Evie's lover is the tall silent type. He is also handsome and will soon graduate as a doctor. Evie has been assured that he will make an excellent husband. He will be a good provider, he will produce intelligent children, he will always be handsome, and, best of all, he is Jewish. Everyone is so pleased. Evie's former lover was Greek Orthodox. Their time together was severely curtailed by the regular lectures she was given on 'The Problems of Mixed Marriages'. Georgio was already married, however, Evie wisely omitted to impart this information to her parents. They were relieved when that liason ended. But anxious too. Evie, their Evie, was then 23, a little too independent, and single. Then the present one happened along. Ah, the joy! the pleasure! Their Evie, their daughter, was going out with a Nice Jewish Boy. They spoke on the 'phone, they wrote their relatives overseas, they bought Evie new clothes, and they watched and waited. Evie, too, watched and waited. For the passion, for the blossoming, for the bells, for IT. However, very little happened. The Jewish lover was the same as the Greek lover only less furtive. The Greek lover was the same as the one who went before only more aggressive. Evie discussed this with Connie. Connie was exasperated, "Will you ever learn?" she said, and then marched off to have dinner with dark and dazzling Dorothy. As for Evie, she had 42 dinners with her new lover. They are presently engaged in number 43.

The waitress approaches their table and places the plates between the cutlery. They take their knives and forks and begin to eat. Evie uses a fist grasp to hold her knife and fork, her lover holds his knife like his father does, as if it were a pencil. This has always irritated her, however, she has not commented on the habit. She concentrates on her steak. Thick and medium rare. The Bearnaise sauce is just right, creamy in colour and consistency. She eats slowly with enjoyment. Her lover however, eats in much the same way as he drives his car. Despite his delicate hold on the knife, he eats as if engaged in some competition. He attacks the food, grinds it to the fork, masticates at least 24 times per mouthful, simultaneously prepares the next mouthful, swallows, fills the cavity again as the previous contents hurtle towards the upper end of his oesophagus.

Evie does not yet realise that her lover regards all meals that he shares with her as hors d'oeuvres. Course one, two and three are the appetisers, she is the main course, to be served thinly on a bed of comfortable springs. Succulent, with excess fat trimmed off. Evie has been her lover's gastronomic delight 42 times.

Evie's lover has finished his meal. He sees the pinkish swirls of blood on Evie's plate. There is a place for blood and that is inside bodies. He should know, he is a medical man after all.

"How can you eat meat like that?" he asks for the 30th time since their relationship began. (Evie has ordered fish 13 times). She soaks up some of the liquid with a piece of meat, pops it into her mouth and smiles as she chews. She will not answer him. Neither will she hurry. She likes to eat.

Evie is thinking. It is about 10 o'clock. She can't be sure. It wouldn't do to look at her watch, and in this dim lighting it's impossible to see the time with a cursory glance. It can't be much after 10.00. They should finish within half an hour. The drive to his house should take about twenty minutes. Forty five minutes for sex and coffee, and another twenty minutes to drive her home. It will be almost midnight before he leaves her place. Evie had said she would have supper with Connie if it were not too late. If the sex and coffee with her lover were omitted she would be home quite early enough. She eats a mouthful of beans garnished with almonds and ponders. She could say she is tired. Or perhaps a headache. She doesn't want to upset him. She's never upset him, not once. In fact, they do not even argue. They get along so well people say, and Evie supposes they are right. It's not as if she doesn't appreciate him or this beautiful meal, she does, and she doesn't want him to think otherwise. And it's not his company she's rejecting, rather it's Connie's she is preferring. But she couldn't tell him this, he wouldn't understand. Besides, he hates Connie. Strange that. Evie thought they would be quite pleased with each other's company. But right at that initial meeting it all went wrong. He surveyed Connie: noted her swagger, her sprawling legs as she sat in the chair, her roll-your-own cigarettes, her glass of beer, her buxom thighs, her scruffy clothes, and dismissed her as 'a bad influence' on Evie. Connie saw his clipped beard, his six foot of trim body, his glass of lemonade, his ever-mobile mouth, his pompous words, his supercilious brow, and decided he was a waste of time. "An inadequate specimen of a less than adequate species" she said. And she hasn't changed her mind. No, if Evie wants to see Connie later on, the truth is definitely not possible. The problem is that Evie and her lover always have dinner, sex and coffee, and now she wants to alter the arrangement, ever so slightly. It shouldn't be so difficult. If he didn't require so much assurance, so much protection, it would be easier. But she shouldn't complain, he's a good man. "He's a good man," they all tell her.

Evie is growing anxious at her thoughts. She is feeling guilt. She is being unfair. She must stop.

"Dessert?" she asks with a smile.

"I thought I might miss it tonight darling," he looks at his watch, "But you go right ahead if you want it."

"There's chocolate mousse on the menu." How he loves chocolate mousse!

"Oh, okay."

He beckons to the waitress. She takes their order and removes the dinner plates.

"How about coffee at home." A statement. Evie gives a non-committal grunt. He is satisfied.

Conversation is unnecessary as the wait for dessert is brief. The chocolate mousse is rich and light. It dissolves in the mouth. It disappears quickly. Too quickly. Evie cannot think, her mind has rejected language. Instead, scenes flicker past. She glimpses herself and Connie seated at the kitchen table. They are drinking port. Evie's lover does not like port, it wrecks the liver. But Connie and Evie like it. Connie and Evie drink it, poured from a cheap bottle with a screw-top lid. They are sitting at the table sipping port and talking. They sit forward in their chairs, leaning towards each other so as to hear every word. The atmosphere is intimate, exciting, compelling. The picture flashes in a fraction of a second. It is, however, very clear. Then another image. She is lying on her lover's bed. Naked. His body is stretched over her own, his cauliflower tongue is in her mouth. Evie gags on the chocolate mousse.

"Anything wrong?" His voice is sharp, he cannot abide bad manners.

"I want to go home." Whose words are these? "Now."

He speaks carefully.

"Are you sick?"

"No."

"Well, what's wrong?" His voice is low, a sort of hiss. "Surely you owe me some explanation."

He's right, she does. But what can she say? 'Not tonight darling'? No, that wouldn't do at all. Perhaps she has been too hasty.

"Well?" he prods at her, "Well."

"I just want to go home." After all, is it such an unreasonable request? Why should she have to explain? But then, on the other hand, he has done nothing to her to deserve this, this rejection.

"I'm sorry," she murmers, "Do you mind?"

"Mind? Mind! Why should I mind?"

He looks at her briefly. She notices that he has drawn in his cheeks, it makes his mouth look mean. He looks away first. Silently, he gestures for the bill, pays it and rises. He goes to the door of the restaurant, hesitates a moment with his hand on the knob, and walks out in front of her. It is not often that Evie has viewed his clothed back, he must be upset. She's sorry, it was not what she intended. It's not too late to change her mind. She stands back as he opens the passenger door of the car. She enters the cabin and looks up. There is doubt on her face. But before her action is completed the door is slammed. She hates car doors being slammed. And now he's revving the engine, she hates that too, and he knows it.

He puts the car into gear and they jerk forward. Evie stares through the window at her side. She is incredulous at what she has done. She said no, she actually said no. She feels remarkably good. But he doesn't. He's behaving like a child. She's never seen him this way before, but then she's never spoken her mind before. It always seemed wiser to remain silent. But now? She feels good, but what about tomorrow? He's a nice man, 'the perfect mate', he does his best. She glances across at him. Maybe I could do it all she thinks. Short sex and coffee with him and still have time with Connie. She opens her mouth to speak. Simultaneously her lover slams the gears into third and with a burst of speed that aggravates Evie he asks,

"Are you sure you're not sick? A headache maybe?" Evie holds on to her seat.

"Yes, I'm sure." The traffic lights ahead of them change to amber. He ignores them and speeds up through the intersection. Evie lights a menthol cigarette. He looks across at her, grimaces, and opens his window. She knows that smoking irritates his hay fever; she never smokes in the car. But generally she has no free right hand. This hand is accustomed to lightly stroking his left leg as he drives. Tonight the leg is untouched. It moves a fraction as he sniffles. God, she wishes he'd blow his nose instead of sniff. He says it's his hay fever, but it sounds so awful. She expects he can't help it. It's not his fault. Everybody has their idiosyncracies and one of his is sniffing. Evie stubs her cigarette. She feels she's been unfair. It would be for the best if she were to admit to a momentary loss of reason and let bygones be bygones. She is formulating her apology when his voice breaks the silence,

"You're acting like a child."

A child! Me? when he's sniffing and careening through the traffic, wrecking the gearbox and slamming doors. Breaking traffic laws. His behaviour is quite extraordinary. I've always regarded him as so gentle and understanding. It goes to show you can never be too sure about anyone or anything. And yet, it seems harsh to dismiss him on the basis of one altercation. Perhaps she should try to talk with him, ask him to explain his reactions. But before she has a chance he is speaking again,

"Look, I think I know what's best for you. I've decided you must be sick. It's the only possible explanation for this irrationality. It's so unlike you Evie. You're usually so agreeable, so feminine. That's what I've always liked about you."

"You sound like my father."

"Nothing wrong in that. Don't forget, I am older than you."

"By ten bloody months."

"There is absolutely no need to be vulgar. Are you going to let me help you or not?"

Evie is silent.

"Listen Evie, I'm a reasonable man, but I'm losing my patience."

"I do not want to go to bed with you tonight." There, she said it.

"Ah, that's it! You've got your period."

"Oh god." He forgets the bleeding trickled off when she started on the pill.

"That's it, isn't it Evie? Menstrual cramps!" He is gleeful, finally, a solution. THE solution.

"No," her voice is steady, "That's not it. I do not want to go to bed with you."

"Well then, that's it. If you refuse to be sensible then I refuse to be reasonable." He draws in his breath, "What in the hell has got into you?"

"I-"

"No, don't answer, I don't want to know."

He turns the car around a corner hitting the curb on the way.

"Will you let me off here please." Connie's house. Her bedroom light is on. He skids to a halt. He is furious. She tells him she will ring him tomorrow. He glares at her. She closes the car door gently and hurries towards the house. She calls to Connie. Her friend comes to the window, sees the car disappearing at the end of the street then looks at her watch. She smiles,

"It's about bloody time."

## Paradise Lost

The day is cool. Inside, the cafe is crowded. The tables scattered across the courtyard to the rear of the dining room are unoccupied now. The sounds from within are muffled by the ragged autumn winds that wrestle in the enclosure. Crisp brown leaves huddle, hushed and crinkling, against the palings of the fence. Some lie trapped in the spaces of the wooden boards of the table-tops. Others drift to the ground where they are whisked over the brick pavement and hurtled against the mounds along the fence. Overhead, the twisted vine grips the trellis, breaking the joins here and there. Without its leaves, the vine appears dead. The wooden boughs have thickened, a thick darkened bark covers even the most slender of the branches. Looking up, the trellis and vine construct a leaded framework for the sky beyond. All manner of greys can be seen there. In the western corner the sky is streaked, so carefully streaked, with a dark layer spread across a lighter one, and then, a little higher, a light one again. In the south, the picture becomes an oil-washed turbulence, a Turner in greys. Toward the east, the sky whitens, bulging into mammoth criss-crossing arcs. Crossing the framework still further to the northern sky the greys are dirtied with yellow fumes from the city. It reminds Julia of the Chagall windows in New York. She places her caffe latte on one of the smaller tables and sits down.

A woman sits at a table in an otherwise deserted courtyard. From the room nearby streams a gaggle of voices. The woman is Julia; her face is averted from the noise. She leans back in her chair, raises her flexed legs, holds them suspended by a knot in her lower abdomen and then brings her knees to rest on the table's edge. The cross bar of the chair digs into one of her vertebrae. She rotates her torso. Now she is comfortable.

The coffee is warm inside her body. It sinks to her stomach smoothly, sensitising the cavity with its heat. The coffee spreads to the stomach walls. Julia returns the cup to the saucer, steadies it and withdraws her fingers from the handle. Now her elbows balance on her thighs, and her palms mould a vessel for her chin. She is waiting for someone, perhaps a friend. Julia is waiting, composed. Julia is occupied. Julia is thinking. What is Julia thinking? Julia thinks of violence and silence, of cliques and gossip, of dishonesty so veiled that you see it as the truth. Julia talks with the woman in her head, the woman who confirms Julia's solitude. During the hours of daylight the florid, intense face of the woman appears to her. Julia closes her eyes to converse more freely.

— Such clever women these I know. Such wondrous words to justify their inaction. They speak of caring, they offer love. But what do they do? Just take me in their arms and silence me with kisses. No-one listens. My voice frightens, my silence brings relief. They distort me, betray me. "Speak to me," she said the other day, "I care," and with my first words she walked over me. Even her backward glance couldn't show me crumpled on the ground. We're growing older. Older and fickle and superficial. We don't hold on to one another, no support, just escape politics in hand. And what about me? I'm running with my own bag. Morality is a heavy heavy sack. They won't listen. They turn their eyes away, take me in their arms, stroke my hair and silence me with kisses.

— I don't want to go to bed with you.

— The personal is political. Made sense back in 1970. A mere ten years and the personal is the sexual. Fucking won't change the world. Fucking is just fucking, no more. I talk to you with trust and you suggest we go to bed together. I risk all that is important and you invite me to stay the night. I ask for some understanding and you pull me to the couch. I write a book that you refuse to read because it is too personal. The personal is political. One reveals the other. You reject both.

— Indolence, that's what I see. Lie in bed till lunchtime, a snack and the newspaper until 2.00, fiddle until 5.00, a drink at the pub, Joan Crawford until 10.30, the late night movie until 12.30, fuck until 2.00, sleep for nine hours. All that wasted rhetoric and a few solitary runners.

Julia drinks from her cup. Her eyes are open. The words have stopped. The face of the woman in her mind lingers. Its flesh is looser these days. We are older now. But whilst our smiles have loosened our words have sharpened.

— She fills my empty shell.

Julia dismisses the face from her mind and drinks again. The coffee is finished. She pushes the cup and saucer to the centre of the table, lifts her knees from where they rest on the edge of the table and allows her legs to collapse on the ground. They are aching. With one foot she hooks the leg of the chair on the opposite side of the table and draws it in closer. She lifts her legs again and places them on the chair. She turns her body to the other side, a slight movement, and feels the chair scrape that same vertebra as she twists. She summons the woman into her imagination.

— Politics! Such facade. What politics are these that attach to lethargy and feather cushions. Can one be political over a continuous round of pasta lunches and curry dinners and midday hangovers. Where's the revolution in dope and mysticism, in pre-history and mother goddesses. Such a lot of noise and I'm straining to hear a whimper.

Julia is tired. Her shoulders have collapsed around her chest. The backs of her knees hurt from their extended position. She glances at her wristwatch. Her friend is late by twenty minutes. This friend is new. This friend wants to know Julia. This friend arranged the meeting five days ago. This friend cannot help.

— Goodbye new friend. I prefer the old and functional delusions.

The courtyard of the cafe is not popular in winter. It is too cold outside. There are nine tables that are not occupied for four months of the year. The income of the restaurant is significantly reduced during these months.

## Morning Absence
### – a documentary

My body is bulbous. A slim neck into a burgeoning hump. A carafe. I am a carafe of red wine. Ageing, but not improving. Stagnant. Once there was promise, now, only a bitter-harsh taste and a muddy residue.

Today, I/carafe recline in bed. Over and around me is a quilt, blue and billowing. It clings to my neck, floats over my body, dips at my feet. The feathers sink and rise and sink and rise, on and on from one edge of the bed to the other side.

Feel the rhythm? It sickens with its softness and undulations. Senses are blunted by the incessant rocking. I need a hard line. Imagine the clean stab of a sharp knife. I take the handle and guide the instrument through the flesh of my thigh. Neat and incisive. The skin divides to reveal a raw blue chasm. There is no blood and it does not hurt.

I must break this monotony. A thought squeezing through my brain would suffice, but I can only draft its jagged trek, I cannot feel it. My neck constricts in irritation. I feel the tidy pounding of the pulse in my throat. Its insistence mocks my blandness. My muscles, my skin, my glands, my organs, my nerves, my vessels are severed from the world outside. All I experience is deficit: nothingness and a froth in my throat. That's hardly enough to keep a person alive.

I feel nothing. I am absent.

I raise my left arm from the bed to my thigh. I claw the skin with my fingers. My skin is numb and annoyingly smooth. My hand remains a protuberance of my thigh. The quilt marks the spot with a hillock. Otherwise, nothing.

My eyes are open so I look through the window. I see leaves and branches and electric wires. The red tiles on the roofs of the houses gnaw at the lichen that huddles in the hollows and crevices. The white curtains in the wall-face are dull.

A fool. I am a casual, unstudied fool. I will not hate myself, I refuse to be tempted by emotion. Emotion distorts the red of the roofs, the green of the trees, the visibility of electric wires. Emotion persuades lichen to adhere to tiles. Emotions direct choices. I remember that. I've read it. I am obsessed with reading. But excessive bundles of words have the punch of a uterine bath. They float around me and in me: my life support. I do not have the courage to turn them off. I do not have the knowledge to halt the stream.

I concentrate on my breathing. If I breathe deeply the air will penetrate my body's surface, fluster the fine hairs of my skin. But this is not successful. The air suffocates me. Locked inside, it is aimless. I am forced to cease. The deep breathing accentuates the tedium. I am a negation.

I close my eyes. I see my eyelids. They are black. I withdraw my left hand from my thigh and cup it over an eye. The blackness does not alter, I only imagine that it should. I plug my ears with my index fingers, there is a rush of fluid that subsides to a cloud. I remove my fingers and the cloud still remains.

I am losing patience.

I realise I am continuous with the bed. If I were separate I would feel the crisp cotton of the sheets, the light weight of the quilt, the foam of the pillow moulded to my shoulders. There would be coloured shapes behind my eyelids, a moving picture through the window. I would hear the screams of the woman next door as she struggles with her son, the sobs of the daughter when she hides from her father. But, as I am, I know none of this. I exist, of that I am sure. I believe I am a made-up bed, inside of which is a gigantic carafe stained with a residue of red wine. I have developed: I/carafe am also a bed.

I cannot tolerate this void, this absence. I must manipulate it.

First Attempt.

> You walk by my window but that's life. You disappear from sight at the door of my house. The noise of the doorbell reaches my ears. At last I am startled. There is a curdling in my stomach, a shudder on my skin. My limbs are paralysed. If I could rise from this bed, walk to the door and open it, I would find you there. I cannot move. You are a caller,

but there is no answer. Shatter the window, leap through, ignore the screech of broken glass upon your skin. Give me a different silence, intense and inspiring. The sound at the door hustles my passivity.

If you want something ask for it.

Second Attempt.

I close my eyes and feel the taut skin on my neck and ribbed chest; The corrugations roll under my fingers. I create channels between the bones. The spaces hurt and comfort. I am reclining, my breasts curve into the softness of the innerside of my arms. Suddenly I feel a fist or a cannonball crash into my breastplate and spring away. The shock steals my breath. Then, irregular panting. Soon the viscera recovers from the blow. But it was there.

Third Attempt.

There are footsteps on the passageway. The touch is firm. Here is a person at my bedroom doorway. Her facial expression adjusts from cynicism to relief. She sees I am alone. Her eyes hurt me they encase so tightly. Down the sheath formed between our two bodies hurtle minute impulses. I move. She sees my smile and walks towards me crumpling the sheath in her path. Like the lie of a breast on the innerside of an arm, I rest.

My windows are dirty.

Fourth Attempt.

You lie on the strip of bed that is alongside me. You are motionless as my hands course your flesh seeking the lines that divide skin from skin and curve from curve. I touch with a novice's wonder. This is the first time of many that I have touched you. You are by my side, silent and still as a statue separated from its pedestal. You are thinking that you are immune to my caresses, that, of course, this will be tedious. How soon, you wonder, will you have to move so as to shake off my grasp. But I persevere, knowing you will stop me when we are both convinced of my failure. You've done it before. The minutes pass. Now your body feels different.

The barriers beneath your skin have dissolved. I press with my fingertips and feel the muscles sigh. When the clock stops and only your breathing marks the time you turn your face towards me, understanding for the first time.

Life is stressful; can I be blamed for these small absences?

Hours gone. Now it is midday. I always wanted to live with you. (We have passed my window together, I watched from my bed. We were laughing. Our arms were linked at the elbow. The muscles of our cheeks were unclenched. We managed to converse.) It was all so long ago.

I must clean my windows but I'm unable to find the implements. Soon the glass will blot out the sky.

The telephone rings, itching my skin. Then a contraction deep deep in my guts followed by a diffuse tingling through my abdomen. I do not try to rise from the bed. The noise stops. This silence is different, it scrapes at my body's exterior creating welts on the skin. None of it is distasteful. The tracks that creep across my surface efface the carafe. If there is no container I cannot feel empty.
"I must be happy; it's not as lively as I would have thought."

# BARBARA BROOKS

## Friday Afternoon

There's a wedge-shaped piece of light that comes in under the bamboo blind, past the fern, and falls on the white tiles above the bath. The radio is playing in the bedroom. Outside, it's winter, and the leaves are falling off the grapevine and blowing about like old newspapers. I like the house in the quiet afternoons, I like the empty house. Still places, light on water, what is it? Something comes back in the quiet that we have been chasing in words for months.

I can remember so much, the mood, the weather, the way light comes into the room. A fly crawling up the wall. But the words escape me.

It's all right, he says, in my relationships people only say something significant about once a year.

I laughed. What could I say?

## An Unfinished Story

> *"In the company of others women always app-*
> *eared to him as more or less out of focus...*
> *because they were continually changing in their*
> *own regard as they adapted themselves to the*
> *coercions and expectations of the others*
> *around them."*

John Berger, *G.*

The kitchen of the old house is large and cool with a tiled stone floor and a bricked-in fireplace; the window looks out on a leaning paling fence and the blank wall of the house next door. There is a Chilean poster over the mantelpiece, next to the dying ivy. The teapot, a jar of sugar, and an ashtray are on the table. The room is cool in summer; in winter they run through to the bathroom, feet striking ice on the cold tiles. There are never enough chairs for visitors, but the life of the place ebbs and flows from the kitchen.

The front of the house looks out over the park, the lights strung out at night under the black trees; the front of the house induces contemplation, conversation drifts away into the large and welcoming space of the view. The kitchen is enclosed; this is the place for talking and planning the day's events, over meals and cups of tea, coming and going. In the mornings they come and go from the kitchen and bathroom, between the steam and burning toast, checking the clock, checking the radio. Kate has an internal alarm system, and wakes up cued in to the news. Lou's timing is more idiosyncratic. Toast in hand at five to nine she says calmly, I'm going to be late again. Kate looks up as the door slams and the gate creaks.

* * *

They are sitting at the kitchen table in the evening, halfdressed in the summer heat. Smells of cut grass drift in from the back yard. Somewhere a radio is playing, and voices hang in the air like smoke. The day has been hot and still but now a quick wind rises and blows down the hall, and slams the door shut, and leaving the smell of a coming storm, faint but unmistakeable.

What is it, Lou has just been saying, one leg thrown over the arm of the chair, that makes me feel so nostalgic about suburban back-yards?

Knowing you'll never own one, Kate says, reaching for a cup of cold tea.

They look at one another across the table.

* * *

The first night Lou comes home with Ben they go straight to her room. She doesn't notice if Kate is there or not. The next night they go to the kitchen. She watches Kate talking to him, that animation which is quite indiscriminate. Then they go to her room and she forgets about it.

The underground currents are rearranging themselves around different fields of force. Polarities. She feels like a magnetic needle, quivering towards her own north, then drawn away. Her skin is alive, she can feel electric currents in her body, she feels a charge every time her heels hit the ground. As if the currents that flow between her body and Ben's store up electricity on her skin, so that she gives off small charges of static electricity when she touches things — stones, earth, clothes.

* * *

Things are changing. Lou is out a lot now; so is Kate, she notices. Often she stays at Ben's place. Once she finds herself on the phone to Kate, they are arranging to be home on the same night.

Kate comes home one night from a dance in a state of suppressed agitation. She has been with John, but is not sure what is going on. Lou remembers John watching the women they know; he has an appraising, no, exploratory, look. When they talk about him, it is as if Kate puts him aside deliberately in order to survey the ground.

* * *

Lou has plunged in. She is taken over. Her room stops looking as though she lives there. She stares at blank sheets of paper. She is no longer aware of the way the shadows move, the way light falls into the room at different times of day.

Together, she and Ben look so hard into one another's eyes they can see each other reflected there in miniature. Watching without moving.

Sometimes when she comes back to her room on her own, she feels as if a vacuum cleaner has sucked everything out of her mind, all the delicate structure of thought, leaving a cage of bone to fill slowly with flesh and blood. When she is alone in the room, it is bare; when they are both there, it recedes, it is nothing but a shelter to keep out the weather. The books lie on the shelves, clothes and dead leaves blow about on the floor.

But she is happy.

\*   \*   \*

What is happening to the men? Lou and Kate sleep close to them, hear the heart, become familiar with the shape of their bodies and their faces. Spend hours talking in the dark. Ben says, what is happening to the men I know, the women are changing, where are the men? Are they still going to the pub, are they still driving around in big cars, are they getting married, going to strip shows, being made redundant? Nobody changes unless they have to, Lou says.

Something is changing but is not yet in balance?

What do the men talk to one another about? Ben and John talk about work, politics, music.

\*   \*   \*

What do Lou and Kate talk about? Work, politics, themselves.

Kate is watching, waiting for a chance to talk, Lou doesn't notice. She remembers the conversations they had at two in the morning, drinking tea and running out of cigarettes when everyone else was asleep. There is this time when everyone lies on the floor, looking at the lean ascetic bamboo blinds, head full of Lessing and Woolf, saying, every time I start talking I end up talking about relationships. It's a career. The time comes and goes, the rooms change, it feels like an extended adolescence; somehow, they think, for other people these things are settled, for me they are continually changing.

They had agreed it was easier to be on your own, to be whole, and not compromised. But the meaning of whole changes. Whole, hold, holding on. Lately, Lou has been saying, if you want it to work ..... Kate is watching.

* * *

Lou goes to the mountains, visiting; and comes back realising she has been turning things over in her mind, without reaching any conclusions. Do the conclusions get filtered out before they reach the surface?

She rings Ben and he says he will come over later. Goes to get a cigarette, but Kate and John are deep in conversation and hardly notice she is there. Goes to bed and waits, hearing every car that turns the corner.

This is the classic: woman waiting for her lover. She gets up and sits at the desk, drinks whisky. How do you get through this mood? Go through to the other side. It comes up, pack it down, pack it down. It comes rising up again, push it down, go through. Eventually, the curious directionless energy worn out, she falls asleep, book on the pillow, light on, ashtray beside the bed. Is awake, every nerve alert, the moment Ben is in the room, thinking, what time is it, and hating herself. He has been talking to Kate and John.

And then what happened? He held her and the other things went away.

* * *

Kate goes away for a week, on a story. When she gets back, she goes straight to Lou's room. It's still early. Lou gets up, puts her arms around her, then leads her out of the room, automatically protective of Ben sleeping.

The two women in the kitchen, talking and burning toast. Kate is on edge and only beginning to unwind. She has been staying with another journalist, working with him during the day, and fading into the corners at night while he entertains his women friends.

I felt like a stick, she says. You begin to wonder what you are. In the daytime I'm trying to work with him on this story, right, we're just two journalists, two human beings, then at night there's this weird situation that I don't fit into at all, this woman sizing me up, and he's treating me so differently that I'm beginning to wonder who's the freak. Talk about confusing. I began to feel as if I was shrinking, there was less and less of me there.

Ben comes into the room and Lou's attention drifts.

I thought he put the word on me one night, Kate says. I can't be sure. I had to handle that one carefully or I wouldn't be able to work with him again. You can opt out of the sexual stuff at work if you can come home at night to people who treat you like a human being.

*       *       *

The kitchen is clean but empty; Lou comes home to find stale bread, vegetables sprouting palely in the baskets. They come and go like visitors. Kate is busy and looks harassed. Lou is still hovering on the edge of some large area of confusion, like a pool of water whose bottom is not visible. The poster has come unstuck and flaps mildly in the breeze from the open window.

They are rarely on their own. John comes to visit. Although his approach is delicate, there is still an undertow. At first, Kate finds him attractive in a lost child sort of way, wants to put her arms around him. Ah yes, that one, she thinks. She learns to talk to him. Sitting in the kitchen one day, sewing a button on her shirt, when he comes, she feels her attention to herself and her work change as it is pulled towards him. She tries to concentrate on herself but is pulled back to him in this undertow. She thinks he is probably unaware of all of this. When she tries to talk to him about it later, he wants to understand but doesn't.

When Lou comes in the balance seems better, and Kate can retire back into herself. She notices how intensely Lou focuses on Ben when he is there, the way Ben asks for this, and the way everything else is excluded.

They are often, it seems, pulled away from one another. Except when Lou is wading out, up to her knees in water, trying to call her boats home.

*       *       *

Lou waits to see what Kate does with the conversation. When John speaks, she smiles, waits, and yet is not uncritical. She 'manages' the conversation, at times seems to 'manage' the relationship. She watches herself — a tendency to defer when Ben talks, to give him uncritical approval. Or, sometimes, total condemnation. She gives control to him, to the point where she has to fight to get it back?

It's easier when the four of them are there. The two women no longer make contact with each other in the old way; now they shout across the distances. She is aware that she has to consciously block out Ben to talk to Kate, but not vice versa.

* * *

Lou's job is simple, low-key; she works in a feminised profession. Can I help you, the women ask all day. There are few men, and they move quickly to the top. They don't have to compete.

Ellen:   It's not a bad job. I just sit at my desk all day drinking coffee and waiting for Friday.

Gret:   I have to get up at five every morning to take my kids to my mother's house. I have qualifications from my own country, but they're not recognised here. They won't promote me, they know I have to take time off when my kids are sick.

Harrison: I'm in this job because I was the best applicant. The women have equality here, they get equal pay.

Ellen:   He's a fool. You should have seen the mess he was in when Mary retired. She was his secretary for ten years. She sucked up to him though, I didn't like her.

The men sail past the women on the way to the top. And the women take it out on each other?

Lou works with four women. Beverly, the woman in charge, is difficult. She gives off confusing messages: I want you to like me/ I want you to do as I say. I am one of you/one of them. She is married to a boilermaker. Who runs the household and who runs the shop, Lou wonders. Beverly hovers at her shoulder all day with a nervous giggle, but never gives her any work to do.

Every morning is the same. Ellen waiting for her first phone call, snarling wordlessly at Beryl who is on the phone to the lawyer about her divorce, and who will cry about it at morning tea. Beverly and Gret are fighting about the work. An enormous emotional web expands to fill the room; everything takes so much more energy than it should.

It's driving Lou crazy. She talks to Kate, talks to Ben, thinks of resigning, or getting a transfer on medical grounds. Eventually she goes to Beverly to have it out. If you need me here, she says, you have to give me some work to do, and leave me alone to do it. If you don't need me, I'll ask for a transfer.

Beverly is frightened of her now.

How's it working out now? Kate asks.

It's much better for me now, in a way. But in a way it's not much better for me unless it's better for them as well. She takes it out on them, and we all take it out on each other.

Have you talked to them?

I can't. But I spoke to the bloke who was there before me.

How did he get on?

He liked it. He said they were all very nice to him.

Every day at lunchtime she buys a paper and walks across the clipped lawns. Working at the university is like being rich, even if you aren't. The azaleas are out. The sky is very blue.

\* \* \*

It might be three years ago now, but she remembers lying on this lawn looking at the sky, the same blue, with someone else.

It's best not to be distracted by other people, he said. She was lying in front of the kerosene heater, very stoned and happy, looking out over the water, watching car headlights through the trees. She would drive there on Friday nights, leaving behind the high-stepping trendies in Surrey Hills pubs, with a falafel sandwich in one hand and the wheel in the other, balancing the night, the car, and a state of euphoria. The city slides back behind her. The light flickers on his face. What do you want? he is asking. To be left alone. He has gone to sleep. The kerosene heater runs out; she turns it off and goes to bed. In the morning when she wakes up the sun comes into her room; she feels clean and calm at the centre, and everything is a delight.

\* \* \*

All I want is to live a decent life, she says to Kate. I want to be left alone.

I know, Kate says, but there's a kind of justice that's out of our control.

\* \* \*

Lou catches sight of them in the restaurant mirror. The two women's faces are vivid. We used to flow along, she thinks, you would never have noticed, the colours were all underwater. Now there is a different kind of life on the skin. At times something that seems more urgent pulls at them, and the subterranean flow is diverted. They seem at times less able to look at what is going on. Beside them there is a fishtank, yellow and orange fishes floating in the water, drifting in and out of the light. Around them, the hard bright lights of the restaurant, the sounds of people talking and eating, waiters coming and going with white plates, green salads, red wine. They are talking over and into the hum of noise. Kate is at the end of the table in a red dress, talking, talking. Suddenly they all look like strangers, in a pleasant kind of way. Lou is slightly unfocused by alcohol, looking over her shoulder, not quite facing what is going on.

Outside, the night, the night workers going home. The city curls around their feet like a cat, the black harbour laps at their feet. They step into a warm lighted car that glides along effortlessly, and go home. The lights are on in office blocks like christmas trees, migrant women are pushing vacuum cleaners all night. The lights are off in small houses, the women and children are sleeping through some stranger's dream. The men turn restlessly in their channels of energy. Doors open and close. They slide into cool sheets and warm bodies. Everything should be reflected in the water, but there are only small lights. There are red stars far away, huge explosions that cannot be harnessed. Tomorrow they will wake up and go to work.

# KERRYN GOLDSWORTHY

## Female Friends

Jackie arrives on her bicycle. It's raining, and she's very late. I'm not ready.

"You don't want to go to this party either, do you," she says.

"Of course not," I say. "But you know what'll happen if we don't."

She follows me into the bathroom to talk to me while I have my shower. I can feel her watching me curiously as I tip back my head under the steamy torrent to wash the shampoo from my hair. I have stood and talked thus in her bathroom and know that her body is perfect, smooth and brown even in winter, lean where it ought to be lean and rich and soft where it ought to be rich and soft. Her face, atop this monument, is a surprise. She is younger than me, but not much. My own body is nothing like hers: fair-skinned, over-indulged, abused and tired from too much wine and not enough vitamins, too many cigarettes and not enough early nights. The basic difference between Jackie and me is that I am aware of death and she is not.

I have reservations about Jackie. But she needs me, and this butters my vanity. She needs a mother and I need to be one; the three years between us might as well be thirty. We define ourselves against each other; she cries and I soothe. When she drinks too much, she collapses and demands to be looked after long before she needs it; when I drink too much I am still on my feet and usually yelling long after I ought to be unconscious. She wears the clothes I choose for her; choose, sometimes, not without malice, to emphasise her legs and breasts, the features she is proudest of. I am the one men talk to and she is the one they take to bed; and if I wish it were the other way round it is perhaps because then I would not be so frequently subjected to her full-frontal traumas of aftermath. Yet although she considers me indestructible she also sees me, rather than herself, as the one in the danger zone.

The bathroom interlude does much to upset this balance of power. She sees me for the first time as both vulnerable and threatening, where previously I have always been nothing to her but indomitably maternal. She is shaken by the sight of my naked back and clearly relieved when I dry myself, put my clothes on and brush the water from my hair; now we are ourselves again, she kittenish and anachronistic in a tight woolly turtleneck, me matronly in black. And we are united in our common desire to get out of going to Julia's party.

There is, unfortunately, no getting out of going to Julia's party. It has stopped raining, and Julia only lives three streets away. I lock my door and we walk off down the road.

We should have stayed away. Julia is already mad with us, and Julia is already drunk. She is our workmate, but she pulls rank often by virtue of her thirty-six years, more than ten years older than the oldest of the rest of us. Perhaps this is why she is surprised that, when she has asked the entire staff of the department to her party, only one of them has turned up apart from us. This, and the prodigious quantities of claret it is clear she has already downed, have put her in an ugly mood. Her non-department friends, several of whom I have met and disliked, are sitting or lying in bedroom and kitchen and hall; some are self-consciously smoking dope, others are talking with an arch middle-aged smuttiness that is both tedious and pitiful. Jackie and I, profoundly uncomfortable, begin to feel very superior indeed. "Get yourselves a drink," says Julia, and leaves us to our fate.

We exchange glances and head with one accord for the lemonade, Greg and Richard are hanging round the table, looking unhappy. We grab the boys and are all retreating up the hall to the deserted sitting-room when Muriel arrives, shining, at the front door. We grab Muriel and the five of us go into the sitting room, shut the door, and sit. We drink lemonade, laugh, and hope fervently to be left alone.

But no, the door bursts open. It is Julia's door, after all. Our hostess is now very drunk, and weeping. She takes up her actress stance in the middle of the room and begins to speak very quietly. We know, or I know, that she will quickly ascend the scale to a fully fledged shriek in the course of her recital. We watch her, still and silent in our seats. Julia is enormous, ungainly and bloated from twenty years of unchecked compulsive eating and solitary drinking. She is also witty, intelligent and generous, and as we sit and listen to her climb the ladder of hysteria we are all trying desperately to remember this. The face of her beautiful sixteen-year-old self smiles sweetly down from the top of the bookcase on the demented harridan she has become; the photograph is a merciless mockery of the face that is beginning to scream at us, unrecognisably distorted by fat, petulance, tears, and the fine criss-cross lines of the burst capillaries of the fair-skinned alcoholic.

Her accusations are incoherent, and of course could not be otherwise. We are, after all, guilty of nothing. Why should she be angry with us? WE are the only workmates who have COME to her party. Of course we all know, on a subterranean level of awareness that has no truck with logic, that she is angry with us because we are the ONLY workmates who have come to her party. She tells us how much she has done for us, and how little we have done for her. What she means is that she hates us because we are young and she is not. We have over her the power of youth, of laughter, of turning away.

Turning away is in fact what we begin to do, since by now she is an awful, awful sight. One of her friends comes into the room to see what the shouting is about and she hurls her sodden bulk into his arms. We see that the doorway, and beyond it the hall, are blocked with people. Richard gets up, opens the window, and climbs through it out into the garden. We follow him.

This is what she hates us for. We are the people who can escape through windows when the nights get too old and turgid. We are young, we are healthy, we are hopeful.

All except me, that is. As I wait my turn at escape she catches my gaze with her own swollen, angry eyes, and I'm transfixed. I'm the one, I can see that. I'm the one person in this bunch of infant defectors that she's picked as a prematurely seedy cynic, a spiritual derelict, a sister. "You!" she says, stabbing a trembling finger at me like someone playing Cassandra. "You!"

I climb through the window. Greg is caught on rose thorns and is laughing shakily. Jackie is crying. The five of us trail back to my house; I let the others in and shut the door behind me. The place has never looked so nice.

The three youngest are the most visibly upset. Jackie is having a violent reaction to Julia's violent performance; she has been listening to the same damning, illogical, vituperative tirades from her mother for as long as she can remember. Richard, the vague and halo-headed lover of all things transcendent and ephemeral, is pale with disbelief at the ugliness of what we have seen. Richard shares with Keats the conviction that truth and beauty are all ye need to know on earth; I have never had the heart to point out to Richard that Keats never got to be thirty. Greg, still punching and kicking his way out of the caul of a protracted adolescence, is nonetheless better at pity than the rest of us, and is for once silent in the face of what he has seen as a simple display of human anguish.

That leaves Muriel and me. Muriel is serenely detached, old enough not to be surprised, different enough from Julia not to be perturbed. Muriel has her own weaknesses and badnesses like everybody else, but none of them has a place in the occasion. My own vision of Julia betrayed is too private to share even with Muriel.

Here, now, it is urgently necessary to make some statement about what we have just seen, some counter-declaration of innocence. Accordingly, since Greg has suggested it and everybody, oddly, is hungry, I make hot Milo and toasted Vegemite sandwiches, and we have a picnic. But Jackie is still in a state, and Greg gets the bright idea of deliverance by mock encounter-group. "Now, we'll re-create it, act it out," he says. "Jackie, lie down." Jackie lies down, there being nowhere else, on the floor. Greg gestures to me. "You be Julia," he says.

I flinch. Muriel is watching from the chair where she's curled up graceful as a cat. She raises one eyebrow at me in bright mockery and I accept the challenge and fling myself into the role of Julia, improvising wildly. It isn't difficult, but I need to concentrate, and soon I'm wholly oblivious to the presence of the others.

Then I hear myself hit a particular note and freeze in horror. Jackie, still on the floor, is laughing hysterically; the boys are clapping; Muriel is looking at me incredulously. It's Greg who speaks. The others turn to try to shut him up, but it's not possible to shut Greg up. "But that was BRILLIANT!" he shrieks."You sounded EXACTLY like her!"

"I know, Greg," I say. "I know."

## Being on Time

Once there was a tribe of American Indians with whose language the anthropologists had a great deal of trouble. The difficulty, it seemed, was tenses. The code was finally cracked when it was discovered that the present tense was the only one they had; the tribe's sense of time was not linear, but cyclical, and time was only the loop of seasons, a net repeatedly cast out and drawn in by the steady hand of a single everlasting summer.

It is still hot, and there is a faint hiss from under the window where someone has turned the sprinkler on the lawn. A telephone is ringing in the upstairs flat.

Evening, morning, flowers open and close, you wash your hair, watch the water spinning down the drain, opening and closing your eyes, washing your feet, the hollow between the ankle bones, your arms, the white stretch with the blue veins, down from inside the elbow to the wrist.

Midday, blinds shut against the heat, lying on the sofa with your feet dangling down and your dress hitched up, reading *Dubliners*. Late evening and you organise your luggage for a long phone call: cigarettes, matches, ashtray, glass of wine, cushion for your elbows, as you lie on the floor and dial the distance code. Nine a.m. and you wash the kitchen floor in a ragged pony tail and borrowed shorts; mark after mark disappears under your cloth and there's a clean smell left behind. Mid afternoon and a friend comes tapping softly, sits with her wine like a small hibiscus blossom on the sofa while you choose piano music and hug your knees in a listening chair. One a.m. and you close down like a station, hesitating on the threshold of your bedroom, the curtains blowing in, the room so full of air and softly lit that you draw breath as on the first sight of the body of some new lover, or before you dive: this is a space that no one can inhabit but yourself. You have washed the walls, painted the furniture and made the curtains, and sleep comes easily. Mid morning and a loud knock; somebody arrives and leaves again, drinking laced coffee and talking fast in the space between. Midnight, sitting at the sewing machine, matching seams and patterns with the window open and the coffee and the cigarette teetering on the mantelpiece, and the music up loud, a gravelly West Coast rocker with long shiny hair. Late afternoon and you have fallen asleep and wake to knocking; someone has come unexpectedly to fetch you, and it's only five minutes to wash your face and dress yourself and then you're out and down into the streets where the sun is setting and the coloured lights are coming on, and the house will wait for you happily without complaint; no arrangements need be made.  Late morning and you try to read, waiting for letters, running out in bare feet down the red brick steps and past the oleander tree, looking up and down the street.  Not quite dawn and you wake without a reason; you put the coffee on and go out to the balcony to look at the embroidered landscape:  blue streaks in a black sky, loops of gold and silver lights on a distant bridge, little squares and rectangles of yellow from kitchen and bathroom windows where showers and breakfasts are beginning days across the suburbs to the sea.

All the time there's that silence that lets you hear the world's noises:  a child crying four houses away; insects cracking in the grass; the man next door singing in the shower; the rain as it gears up for a storm and the lightning flashes in through the side curtains, trailing thunder.  You go to work, you shop and visit and when you come back, everything's the same.  Perhaps there's a letter in the box.  You throw open doors and windows and turn the music on and then you change your mind and turn it off; books whisper at you.  Pictures sing to you. The weather might change, the phone might ring, the sky might fall; you are calm.  You acknowledge the weather, answer the phone, watch the sky.  You wash a dress and water a rose, you read the papers, you write a list of what you have to do today, you check the calendar on which you have marked the dates of crucial appointments, full moons and birthdays.  You can hear flute music, madrigals, Greek folk songs; you can hear the girl next door as she turns on the water for her morning shower or her evening coffee.  You get out of your own shower and wipe the mist from the mirror, you study your face and dry your hair, sometimes you remember the perfume and some-times you forget.  You seem to buy books in threes.  Black bread is better than the ordinary kind, Red Delicious apples are better than any other kind, orange juice with yoghurt is nice and any kind of cheese at all is better than most other things.  Sometimes the grey cat is lying on the path in the sun, and it will make a pattycake grab with never a claw for a passing ankle or a lowered hand, and roll over to offer its tender underfur to your fingers.  You go out, you come home, you find the gold coloured key in the ring of silver ones, you open the door to white tiles with a green design in the hall and dark wood, and the cool air and the silence.

# ANNA GIBBS

## Having Nothing to Say

I showed a couple of poems to my English teacher once. She'd asked to see them, simply assuming I wrote — I'd said nothing about it. "Well," she said, handing them back, "you have a nice way with words but nothing to say." I didn't argue.

My father, worried when I told him I was going to give up arithmetic, science and geography as soon as possible, demanded what on earth I thought I was going to do without them. "Be a playwright," I said. "So actually I only need English." He began to explain why this was fallacy. My mother, listening, turned her back on the conversation. She had long given up discussing this kind of thing. Finally, seeing words weren't going to make an impression on me, my father decided to take action. He took me to see one of his fellow academics, the head of the Drama department, whom he expected would convince me of the impracticality of my intentions. Not that he wanted to discourage me: merely to set things in a proper context, one he termed broadly 'the real world'.

The professor asked me whether I thought I had anything special to say. "No," I said, feeling foolish. "I just like writing." "Thank God!" he said. "That's the important thing, to love words for their own sake." I left, relieved to have something concrete to report to my father.

When the exam results came out I had failed pretty well everything, except English. "I can't understand it," my form teacher said. "*History*. It's only fiction with a few facts thrown in. Presumably you left out the facts." A lengthy pause. Then: "Haven't you got anything to say for yourself?"

I thought about it. A lot of the appeal had gone out of words.

So I have nothing to say about the stories, really. Except that perhaps it was the tracks of ink irregular over the page that drew them out of me.

"What they call a wank," I tell you now, as my fingers trace scriptural patterns over your breathing breasts, up and down the front of your body. For no reason, really. But as I speak close to your ear you have begun to chuckle softly, your whole body surfacing in ripples. Your seismographic laughter.

# 4 O'Clock in the Afternoon

The sun fills the upstairs room where I work, desk under the window. The objects in front of me: a jar of pens and pencils, books, postcards on the windowsill, a bowl of paperclips, a mug of tea. Their shadows lean over the desk and onto the paper. A replica of the New York skyline on the card by the potplant lengthens toward me.

When it covers the desk completely it will be time to tell myself I have done nothing today. Already I am trying to take stock of the empty maze of hours. Minutes weave through them like the tiny tracks that arrive overnight on the sand dunes. An intricate, aimless pattern appears and disappears as each part of it loses itself in the next. I think of the gestures that made the minutes change into one another without ever adding up to anything. Making tea, lighting cigarettes, listening for the sound of a particular car outside my window, falling into a daydream in the sun, sharpening pencils, looking for things lost on the desk—all those etceteras. This is the body in relation to its own expenditure, I tell myself. This is pure work, work prior to production. Really I know it's waiting.

The day becomes nothing but its own interstices. The void at the centre of things opens. This is the black hole I joke about. "She's a real black hole candidate," I say of someone I don't want to waste time arguing with but wish would be swallowed up forever.

The skyline advances over the desk until it obliterates itself. The warmth leaves the window. The postcard too disappears into formlessness. I don't turn on the light. "You'll ruin your eyes," my mother would say. But something other than vision has taken over.

The void is about loss, yes. Not loss of a particular object. Although you miss her. More, loss of objects altogether.

And this is not recovery of lost time, nor compensation for it. It's a continuation: you intensify the void until something else emerges. The body demands other relations.

## Street Life

Rush hour in the rue de Rivoli lasts all day. You go with the rest, kamikaze from the kerb leaving English tourists like stranded pigeons on the brink of the twentieth century. Their mouths open to take in history. They swallow it whole for lunch. You wonder what they will do for dinner.

*  *  *

The plaques along the quais: Rimbaud lived here, here Villon, on the island someone you've never read. These are absolute and end in full stops at your feet. Not far from here Foucault is lecturing on discursive formations. In the Bourse the telex machines make mountains in waste paper baskets. The boy in the window across the road fires a pinball machine and the figures on the screen above the back of his head change and change again. You write this and as it appears on the page you think you have read it before.

*  *  *

On the other side we hunt pianos in the rue Monge. A sonatina followed by another. You haven't got room for the noise. The street is full of cars and people shout on the stairs. In your room there is laughter. I am teaching you English in monosyllables. You don't know what is what. You don't know New York New York but you like Gertrude Stein Gertrude Stein Gertrude Stein. You say there is not room for all this in your head. You say this over and over. Then you laugh and say something else. Say something else.

*  *  *

I keep telling you it's not the same but I can't tell if you're listening. You're half gone into tomorrow, next week sometime or "when I come to Australia." You turn Australia on your tongue while I watch and it comes out other as the moon. When you close your mouth the white disc disappears down your throat. When you open it again in the dark there are two facing crescents. If I shut my eyes now I will see the last tram running all the way down Bourke St on shiny tracks out of the office block where the moon is about to burst from an upstairs window. When I tell you this you know straight away it's a full moon. But this is my story and I haven't decided what kind of moon it is. Or if I have I'm not telling. It's just a moon. Not the same one you point to now through the dark window.

* * *

I don't mean to give you the wrong idea. I don't know if there are any right ones. For instance the truck that has just passed us: there is writing on its side, but I don't know what it says. Maybe it's a message, destination unknown. How can you tell where something's going until it gets there? There are directions, but there is also a distance, and maybe by that time you've gone off to wash the dishes anyway.

* * *

You're sick of all this. You sit facing the wall and try to ignore me. You begin to write. When words refuse to be marshalled in rows you let them fall on top of one another until your maze of hieroglyphs approximates the shape of the city. Now we are somewhere in Montmartre. The streets are an arabic text. Maps seem beside the point. There is a certainty about being lost you do not want to lose. We could stay all day in this tiny cafe under the arch and no excuse would be needed. The sun arrives between the lines. Suddenly everything is possible. I look around and we've both disappeared.

* * *

Later your postcard arrives. The one we stole from Beaubourg the day I took you to look at tourists. Or perhaps not the same one, but like. Two women, who could be twins, on the back of a hand. Or maybe it's one woman (who looks like you) arm in arm with her image. Which is woman and which is image? Say two images. On an image of a hand. One image on a card. I hold the card in my hand and linger on the footpath, trying to read your mind. My true confessions: wish you were here, I wanna hold your hand.

* * *

On the tennis court in dazzling sun, words come loose. Arriving in swarms, out of the blue. No question of picking and choosing, ordering and sorting. You take what comes and more follows. The ball arcs, bounces, and is gone again. You will run to meet it when it returns from a different direction, flexing your muscles as it meets the racquet. You can't see the other end of the court clearly. You think the ball is on the line. The game will go on, or a new one will start.

# MARY FALLON

## Working Hot

you toss me about toss me around between your hands "not your common garden variety fuck" said Freda Peach I roll my palm back and forth across your pubic hair pudenda rolling soft dough flat on a board I have you dancing on the end of this pin doll I can wind the music box to a torture to a fever pitch I can make you toss and twitch a white boat on a sea of spit a white corpse eyes wide open that old rock and roll washed over and into brought to life with these here electrified wires — ten fingers — in the right place plug into sockets I feel the jolt right up to the eyeballs you have been condemned to the electric chair I am the one with the responsibility to pull the switch but I must admit I am the one whose back arches it is then we are in the thicket together the thickest and tightest part of the night's exercise and I know on this Godforsaken planet in this world of scarcity and lack you lack nothing there is nothing stinting nor niggardly that you are gorged and sated and that I have provided that there is no give and take no economy worth speaking about does the ocean count the number of waves it gives and tick and tote it up against the number returned there is no checkout chick in this bed no invoice or inventory

* * *

that body that Vienna loaf that Camembert that avocado that glaced fruit that marzipan iced fruit cake

you come over and over
so quick
so many times

I'm thunderstruck
I'm flabbergasted
I'm in awe of my fingers
(the tips tingle if we haven't fucked for a few days)
"come and give me a kiss" said Toto
"here and here and here and one here"

"I can't get enough of your mouth" said Freda Peach
and she couldn't

I was a mouse running along a live wire between two terminals
— your hands
you ran me back and forth
back and forth I ran

going to sleep with you holding me saying I love you because . . . .
over and over — and you even had reasons reasons like a contract

"the girl with the magic mouth" said Freda
and I was

                              *   *   *

". . . you could cry like that every day" said Freda Peach cold
". . . do you mean me do you mean I could or one could" asked Toto
". . . anyone could we could all cry like that every day if we wanted
to if we didn't stop ourselves"
". . . come to me" she said
how many people can say that without it sounding ridiculous but she
can Freda can Freda Peach

                              *   *   *

the essence of what is in my hands running through to you in my
mouth batting like a moth tongue around a bulb but breaking the
bulb breaking through to the live wire between my teeth satisfied
(a knack for loving a skill something I do well — well well well good
for me)

such pleasure this morning — pleasure — the word warms my groin
runs circles around my clitoris rings it a noose a festoon that is strung
from the tree in my guts and they strain and bend with a weight as

ponderous as pleasure — pleasure pleasure pleasure singing down through my mouth open onto yours and into yours and your jerked head and your shut eyes your left arm outstretched going down on you is all joy all exploration the eroticism of trust (even respect) saying you you you . . . with my tongue

(where do you hide your knives and the red eyes even going down and coming up I am vigilant for the touch of steel blade of pain you must hide something somewhere we women have all baited booby trapped our bodies I am not naive enough to believe there is no concealed weapon come on now honey let me frisk you)

"Ah I madly love . . . . . " Genet "but fate had ways of opening my eyes or of opening the darkness in two so I could see into it."
— the orgasm the point of intersection the point where all erotica erotic language etc attain that apex of vibrating life (a snapshot — this is me on my wild goose chase)

"then I was filled with the gloom that suddenly comes forth at the approach of death. Our hearts cloud over. We are in darkness."

\* \* \*

waking up arms around your neck and breasts thinking oh shit the washing pay the rent buy the wood for the bench and you wake up and we're kissing and it's so warm and drowsy and I say no no today we won't spend all day in bed today I must do the washing pay the rent get the wood for the table ring about the paint . . . .

"what about the washing?"
"it won't get washed"
"what about the rent?"
"it won't get paid"
what about the table it won't get made
what about the paint it won't get bought

— passion and excess (yum yum)

\* \* \*

bereft stranded beached

*image*
a woman with her legs apart masturbating furiously under floodlights
in an empty stadium

*image*
a swamp being drained

*image*
you deliberately sopping up gravy with chunks of bread

*image*
you treadling determinedly and mechanically on an old Singer
sewing machine the needle stabbing in and out of material under your
keen eye

*image*
the image as tight as a pearl milked from me
realising you're just lazy
"You're just lazy Freda, just a fucking lazy lover"
"Yes I know. It's true. I am."
Toto masturbates
a voyeur rubs her breasts and belly
saying to herself
"It means too much
    divest it
It means too much
    divest it
It means too much
    divest it"


Oh I am bereft stranded beached
your body is then sometimes
such a honeycomb
then
such a rock
I am suddenly
    breaking
        my

teeth
   and
fall back
off you
humiliated

                       *   *   *

"We desire to be desired" says that bitch Freda Peach, "chew me,"
she whispered hoarsely, "chew me."
   and
in my mouth full
my imagination and
imagining full of
a flesh flower

— a fat marzipan rose
— an intricate radish rose

a sex salad
a lucky muff diver
what a lucky licker
muff diver dyke
sportswoman chewer
glutton to some

you say
"You'll never have enough"
   or
"You'd come at anything"
to be full of you
is to be full of myself
like a fat shadow
(here is a secret for you
I have discovered the shadow orgasm)

you fall asleep like a kid with a belly full
apple cores and passionfruit skins
composting at the bottom of the bed

                       *   *   *

at the bottom of the bed
is where your head was

I found a tongue twister
engorged in the tuft of your muff
I stuffed

O.K. now you try it

# GEORGIA SAVAGE

## Flowers

"I found a dildo," Marion hissed, her face an inch from mine. "It was made out of ping-pong balls and a carpenter's tool."

More than anything in the world, I wanted to laugh, but I didn't let myself.

We'd been strolling in the garden, Marion and I, when she saw a yellow carnation. She'd snapped it off and carried it triumphantly inside to stick it in a crowded vase where it disappeared from view. On the way we'd passed her son, the flautist, who was lying, one leg dangling, in the hammock. His hair was tied back with a piece of braid and he was as still as a Red Indian. As we passed him, he turned his head away.

As soon as Marion had disposed of the carnation, she said, "I've got to talk to you about Austin," and she'd backed me against the window and told me about the dildo.

"It was in his car. I got it out and showed it to him and asked him where he got it. He said he'd never seen it before, but I knew he was lying because I found two more ping-pong balls in his handkerchief drawer. They had holes bored in them too."

To stop myself laughing I bent down and scratched a mosquito bite on my foot. As I straightened up, a long shadow beside the window moved and I knew the flautist had got out of his hammock and was listening to us.

I asked Marion how she knew what the dildo was.

"What else could it be?"

I thought for a while, then murmured, "Nothing."

"He'd been using it on that bitch. They go every lunch-time to the river."

"How did you find out?"

"He told me. Not in so many words, of course, but I knew. He came home late one day and I asked him where he'd been. He said he'd been down by the river. Poking about, he said."

Again I wanted to laugh. This time I stopped myself by concentrating on the flautist. "He shouldn't be listening," I thought. "It gives him an unfair advantage."

Marion was waiting for me to say something, so I said the only thing I could think of, "Why would he use the dildo? Why wouldn't he do it himself?"

"Because they like kinky sex. That's why. Austin has always been kinky and I've always known, though I pretended I didn't. Once when Don Larsen was staying here, Austin went to bed early and Don kissed me. He wanted me to go to his room with him, but I pushed him away and made a joke out of it. Then I went towards our bedroom and as I did, Austin came dashing in the front door. He was stark naked. He'd been around by the guest-room window waiting to watch us."

The thought of Austin, who was sixty and shaped like a bull seal, dashing naked through the shrubbery was almost too much for me. Again I stopped myself from laughing by wondering what the flautist made of the conversation.

Marion's jealousy was well known in the district. Austin had always been a stud and Marion had always been jealous. She was frightened to go away, even for a day. When she had a spinal disc removed, instead of going to a surgeon in Melbourne, she had it done by a doctor at the Maryston Hospital. He bungled the job and as a result she walked gingerly like one of those old-time Chinese girls who'd had her feet bound. Needless to say children in the street sometimes copied the walk.

"They've started a sort of club," she was saying. "Austin and that woman. They send away for porn magazines and kinky underwear. Some of the women have taken to wearing crotchless knickers. It's disgusting. Linda Willis told me her husband got a magazine and because it wasn't sexy enough, he returned it and asked for his money back."

"What was it about?" I was agog.

"A man who was in love with his camel. He wanted to screw it, but couldn't because it was so tall, so he had a sort of step-ladder arrangement made which fitted on the creature's rump. He had the ladder padded with velvet so it'd be comfortable on the camel."

Marion turned away from me and blundered into the coffee table, knocking it over.

Ashamed at my lack of sympathy, I rushed to pick it up. "Can I get you something?" I asked. "Make tea?"

"No, I'll make it myself in a minute."

"Then I'll get you a brandy. Where is it?"

She told me and I went into the kitchen and fossicked around for brandy and ice. While I was making the drink, I thought of the film I could make of Marion's life. My version of The Last Picture Show. She was so typical of her generation, she could have been the proto-type. She came out, as they used to say, in Adelaide during the war. Her mother was a tough old autocrat who fancied herself as a com-edian. In fact she ran an amateur concert party which she took touring around the military hospitals. She took Marion too and because the girl was tall for her age and stooped a little, used her as the butt for a lot of her jokes. As a result Marion grew up believing herself un-attractive. When she started going to dances at service clubs and danced with young men on their way to fight in New Guinea, she suddenly found herself a belle. It went to her head and she had a succession of the kind of affairs people had in those days — tangos, orchids crushed against boyish chests and ill-timed ejaculation on organdie evening dresses. Then she married Austin who was in the Army. While they were honeymooning in Tasmania, she told him about the affairs she'd had and he spent the next thirty years punish-ing her.

In civilian life Austin was an agricultural scientist. After the war, his work brought him to Maryston and he and Marion settled there. By then they had two babies, Martin the flautist, and a younger boy whose black humour indicated that he was a throwback to the touring comedian.

Practically the first thing Austin did in the district was start an affair with a journalist called Blanche. With a few pauses the affair lasted for thirteen years, then Blanche married a Queen's Counsel and discarded Austin. That was his first big affair but it wasn't his only one. Over the years he had many lady-loves and made little effort to hide the fact. If anything he went to the other extreme by leaving corny clues, like the stubs of theatre tickets, on top of the dishwasher. Somehow the marriage survived, but his latest romance was with Marion's cousin and apparently the double indignity was more than she was prepared to swallow.

My musing had taken me to the kitchen window. The scene outside was a pleasant one. Spray from the garden hose had made a rainbow and under it a fat grey bird was drinking. I wanted to stay where I was and watch him but another spurt of guilt sent me back to Marion.

She'd composed herself and was sitting on the couch. Her face looked as if she'd had time to touch it up but that must have been my imagination.

As I gave her the brandy, she looked up into my face and said, "Tell me what to do."

"The last time I did that, it misfired. Remember?"

The Gaffney's always had a New Year's Eve party. It was one of the social events of the district. The year before Marion had confided to me that she was too humiliated by Austin's love life to be able to face the festivities. Stupidly I advised her to pretend she had a lover too. I told her to slip out of the house on the night of the party and to stay out for an hour or so. Marion took the advice, but Austin wasn't the type to have his thunder stolen. By the time she got back he'd spirited the guests away. She returned to find the music playing, the curtains moving gently in the breeze but nobody there. That year she saw the New Year in alone.

"It'll be different this time," she told me, then she took a gulp of the drink, put it on the coffee table and to my surprise got up and left the room. She was back so quickly it seemed like a magician's trick. In her hand was a bundle of magazines and it was only later that I realised she'd had them on a table in the hall ready to grab.

"Here," she said, thrusting them at me. "I found these in Austin's study."

The magazines were printed on poor quality paper with illustrations of even poorer quality on the covers. I opened one and read, "Patti had a flat in Bondi. She had red hair and her boobs bobbled when she walked. She lived alone with a Great Dane. His name was Satan. One day her friend, Sue-Ann, visited her. Patti Said, 'Let's fuck with Satan. I do every night, and it's fun'."

I shut the magazine and said, "You aren't really worried about nonsense like this, surely."

I'd hardly got the words out when Marion snatched the magazines out of my hand and hissed, "How would you have liked it if Brook read things like that?"

There was a silence in the room which went on and on. I could smell the roses outside the window but I'd forgotten the young man hiding there. Marion's words had stunned me. Brook read such things! Brook who was beautiful and gallant and honest.

I heard Marion say, "I'll make the tea." Her voice seemed a long way off. Then she left the room. I stood up to go home. Our friendship was over, that was certain. It'd been killed by the mention of a man who'd been dead himself for nearly three years. I took a couple of steps towards the kitchen to tell Marion I was leaving.

A voice said, "You can't be cross with Mother for using Brook as a weapon when you use him as one all the time." It was the flautist. He'd come in without a sound and was standing behind me.

I spun to face him, "I don't know what you mean."

"Yes, you do."

"I don't."

He didn't answer and I said, "You've no right to say a thing like that."

"You've no right to do it."

"Do what? What do I do?"

"Use Brook to keep other men away from you."

"That's the sickest thing I've heard. What about. . ."

He cut me off. "If you're going to mention your friend Duffield, don't. He merely proves my point. You're not interested in him. You couldn't be. That's why you let him hang around. He doesn't threaten your little cocoon, does he?"

I was too shocked to answer. His words, coming on top of the scene with his mother, were more than I could cope with.

He said, "Sit down. Mother's bringing in the tea."

"I can't stay."

"Of course you can. Just calm down," and he turned his back on me, went to the bookshelf, pulled out a book and began to read.

At that moment Marion came into the room. She was carrying a tray loaded with a Bertie Wooster style afternoon tea. Involuntarily I moved forward to help her and before I knew it, I was sitting on the couch holding a cucumber sandwich and a teacup. That's not the whole truth of course. I stayed because of what the flautist had said to me. I was furious with him but I was intrigued as well.

For the next half hour, Marion and her son talked about an exhibition of wood-cuts they'd been to. It was as if neither of the earlier scenes had taken place. While they talked, I watched the flautist. I didn't know much about him and was surprised he knew so much about me. I knew from gossip that he had a habit of getting up at an ungodly hour and standing motionless in the garden to listen to the wind bells in the silver birch. At such times he wore a striped blanket around his shoulders. Some local wit had nick-named him Uncas, after the last of the Mohicans. The name stuck and he was known all over Maryston as Uncas Gaffney. I knew also that he'd given up his job in the orchestra to travel and write music. His music was marvellous. He wrote about two semi-quavers a year, but when he got them down, they were breath-taking. The only other thing I knew about him was that he'd once visited a prostitute in Sri Lanka. As I ate my way through gem scones and walnut cake, I found myself wondering what the prostitute was like. Was she an elegant creature with her own apartment, or was she an undernourished thirteen year old, working in a cubicle in a crowded slum?

As for the things he'd said to me, I put them at the back of my mind. I knew I'd take them out and think about them, later, when I was alone.

When we'd finished tea, Uncas said to his mother, "Let's show Vinnie the Ponds."

I made a feeble protest, but Marion said, "Nonsense, it's a wonderful place. You wouldn't forgive yourself if you didn't see it. I'll go and change my shoes."

Uncas and I drifted outside. As we went along the verandah he picked two pale trumpet-shaped flowers and stuck one behind his ear. He gave me the other one. I was fixing it in my hair when Marion came out.

"How very D.H. Lawrence of you," she said. Her tone was light but I could tell the floral pas de deux hadn't pleased her.

We drove to the Ponds, then got out and walked along a road which was no more than two pale lines in the grass. Marion was right. It was a wonderful place. The road was lined with gums, their trunks were smooth and creamy and their branches met above us. They were so big they must have been five hundred years old. Beneath them were pools of dark water with birds flicking across the surface as they fed on insects. There was so much water, so much shadow, so much growth, I wanted to build a hut and stay there forever. When I said as much, both the Gaffneys bent on me looks of tenderness strong enough to surprise me.

They knew the scientific name of everything – birds, butterflies, even the wildflowers. And they bandied them about as casually as I bandied swear words.

When it was time to leave, the flautist waded through water into a field covered with tiny white daisies. They were light and almost transparent, moving like a sea of silver in the last light of afternoon. He knelt, and looking more like Uncas than ever, picked me a bunch.

He brought them back and as he handed them to me, he trod on a tussock, stumbled and hit me in the breast. He'd been about to say something, but for some reason his poise finally deserted him and he turned his head away and coloured. I grabbed the posy with both hands and tried to look as if men hit me in the breast with flowers every day. I suppose it was a fitting end to an afternoon which had offered more than one moment of comedy.

I stayed at the Gaffneys for dinner. Austin was home and all through the meal he and Marion called each other darling.

She'd say, "Will you have some more pork, darling?" And he'd answer, "No, thank you, darling. Well, just a little perhaps."

Austin obviously liked having two women at the table. At the same time I could see he was irked because the flautist, who was a vegetarian, stayed in the kitchen preparing some food of his own. Austin kept up a series of jokes about health-food fanatics, and whenever he let one fly, he'd lean back in his chair like a mischievous child and his eyes would gleam with satisfaction as he looked from Marion to me and back again. At the end of the meal, though, he seemed to forget I was there. He'd drunk a lot of wine and he began to give Marion looks of the kind of ardour you'd expect to find in crazy old novels like The Sheikh. Certainly I'd never seen anything like them before. Marion must have been aware of them — she couldn't fail, but instead of responding she became quiet and spent a lot of time looking at the tablecloth. Gradually it dawned on me that I was watching a courtship ritual, so as soon as I could, I took my leave.

I walked through the garden to my car in bright sunlight and found the flautist waiting there.

As I opened the car door, he said, "You shouldn't worry about my parents. They have the kind of relationship they want." When I didn't answer, he said, "Most people do, you know."

Still I didn't say anything and he went on, "They have a mother-child relationship. Father does something naughty and Mother punishes him."

"Don't be a nut," I said. "You've got it back to front. Your father does the punishing. He's been doing it for years. That's why he has his tatty little affairs."

"No. That's what everyone thinks, but it's the other way around. It's a game they play. When he's been with another woman, Mother makes him go through a purification ceremony. That's part of the game too and I suppose they both enjoy it."

"Did you learn all this by listening at the window?"

He had the grace to grin. Like most people who don't smile much, he had a beautiful smile. He closed his eyes for a moment first, then opened them and looking straight at you, beamed. He did it then.

I put the car into gear and drove away without speaking again. At the end of the drive, as I turned into the road, I looked back. He was standing beside the silver birch tree. He was watching me, his hands at his sides, not moving at all.

# DOROTHY JOHNSTON

## Mrs. B.

When Mrs B.was still living with her husband she used to spend Sunday mornings at the Scheherezade. On a winter morning, drinking her coffee at one of the front tables, with the sun warming her back. Her husband would talk business out on the footpath with the other men, in their casual clothes, their European cardigans. The footpaths on a Sunday morning were always crowded. She called them the 'Knitwear Brigade', emphasising the 'k' at the front. She could still go and visit her friends. It wasn't that they had rejected her. She'd order latkes for lunch, with schnitzel. The Scheherezade made the best schnitzel in Melbourne. At one end of Acland Street were the continental cake shops, the restaurants. At the other end were the massage parlours.

Theirs was in a back street. In the beginning they were working just to pay the rent. The paint was peeling off the walls. There was a big dip in the floor behind the front door. Denise told Tony they'd better put a sign up to warn the clients. They didn't want any sprained ankles. "And what about workers' comp?" she teased him. But to Tony things really did seem newer, better than they were. He extended this faith in the threadbare tools of the trade to the girls, who, in spite of themselves, were flattered.

Tony took Denise on an introductory tour of the house.

"This will be the African room. Can you see it? Tigers' heads, a drum in this corner." He drummed experimentally on the window-sill. "Wall hangings, coconut mats, the whole bit. Maybe the whole room like the inside of a tent."

"Elephants trumpeting outside the window?" said Denise.

"Right!"

Tony looked at her and shrugged.

Denise made a face at him.

"What's wrong, mate? You're pissed off with me for something."

"Not with you exactly. I don't know," said Denise. "This place gives me the shits. Look at it. It's shit. Falling apart."

Tony came over and put his arms around her.

Denise traced one finger lightly across his eyelids. "You need your glasses cleaned, mate," she said.

They sat in the kitchen with the thin necessity of the smoke around them, with the three tables that Tony had picked up from God knows where, and the bright blue towels with pictures of sea-horses and starfish and sand-buckets that Tony had got cheap from the K-mart.

"But you're supposed to have white towels," said Denise.

"White, schmite," said Tony, throwing back his head and showing them his brown throat. "You want this place to look like a hospital? At the Touch of Class they have towels that match the wall-paper, like they're specially dyed. And there's a chick employed just to do the initials in the corner."

Mrs Bibrowski was filling the electric jug at the sink. She turned and sat down before she said, bravely, to the two of them, "With the coloured towels, it won't be showing so much the dirt."

"Jesus fucking Christ," said Denise.

Mrs Bibrowski came back into the kitchen after doing a massage and washed her hands carefully in the sink.

"He says I have skinny legs, for someone who is fat."

Denise snorted. "You're not fat."

Mrs Bibrowski looked unconvinced.

"Don't take any notice of what they say," Denise told her. "It's all bullshit."

Mrs Bibrowski had the thick, opaque skin of Europeans and large brown eyes, though the circles under them were coffee-coloured. Six grey hairs radiated from a point just above her forehead, like Canberra streets. One of the clients said she was a kind of middle-aged Mary Poppins. Another said that she was unreal. She never swore in English, referring to sex always as 'the extra' or 'the finish of the massage'. Occasionally she would swear softly to herself in Polish. Denise teased her, saying that she 'lived in fairyland.'

She became quite popular with the older clients.

"It doesn't mean a thing," Denise warned her, "when they say they're in love with you and stuff. They all do it."

The clients called her Mrs B. Denise called her Bibby. She had a particularly unkind way of saying it, drawing her lips back over her widely-spaced teeth, with a small quiver at the sides of her nose.

One day Tony appeared with a big bunch of paper flowers. He stood in the doorway, waving them round his head.

"Jesus Christ, " said Denise. "Those things stink like they've been shut up in the dirty towels bag for a month."

"Aren't they amazing?" said Tony. "You should have seen the people in the tram!" He sniffed elaborately and laughed.

The flowers were amazing. They had a kind of lopsided concentration about them, as if in the folded and cut paper there was stored knowledge of all the Roman baths and saunas belonging to the better class of parlour, those Corinthian columns made of stone but smooth to the touch, unweathered, as if things out of nature had stopped ageing too, in a kind of marking time. Sometimes they smelt only of a staleness that had taken away the original and preserved it, but sometimes, in the way they nodded like real flowers in front of the fan, they took up the body smells of the rooms and held them on their frail surfaces like a gift.

It seemed that Mrs B. was gradually getting used to things, beginning to weave herself into the patchwork life of the house. There was a part of her immediate past which she referred to a couple of times at the start, afterwards not at all. It had to do with a dress shop — the first stock after hours of discussion, the overheads inflating in front of her eyes, a recession that she had refused, till then, to believe in. She had almost gone out and dragged people in off the footpath, those who had the unthinkable cruelty to stand at the window and take their fill of looking and never buy. The restraint she had been forced to practise had caused a short circuit somewhere.

She took up her sewing again. She was decorating a shirt with a fist of King Kong. It indicated a kind of settling-in, the way she sewed that hairy and intricate monster's paw, stitches piled on top of each other until it was truly three-dimensional. King Kong held a nubile, red-haired Fay Wray, no expression at all on her perfect Hollywood face.

Denise said she wasn't really embroidering a shirt but making a bird's nest.

"Gniazdko," said Mrs B., "gniazdko," wrapping herself in the soft gravel of her Polish consonants.

She finished the shirt and Tony wore it, accepting the joke, making it his. He teased her about it, with a special look from under his lashes.

It was Tony's normal practice with women to give them a great deal of attention in the beginning. After a while he would feel genuinely that he knew all there was to know about them and pass on to someone else. But with Mrs B., although there was the ordinary flirting, things never really ran their course. Tony was always about to move to a better place, to re-do the rooms, urging them to make more money. He came to regard Mrs B. as a person having hidden talents. It made him feel good to think he had brought her out of her depression.

In the rooms where only the clients could follow her she would arrange the paper flowers on the mantle-piece, hesitant and flushed, a hostess before a dinner party, then stand to one side to deliver her speech. If the client was a migrant like herself she would sometimes have more to say, giving him the benefit of the doubt. Then it would re-appear suddenly, with the force of a thousand horsemen riding into the Baltic, a vision of exactly where she was.

When the client touched her in his special, impersonal hurry, instead of flinching like the younger girls, giving him a cold look, though hers wasn't exactly warm and she didn't exactly open her legs to him, she would lie there under the paper flowers, giving her shoulders a little hump. She straightened them in an unconscious movement from her childhood, becoming, under his eyes, in the moment before he put his cock inside her, if not quite a schoolgirl, then not quite a woman either. A transparent smile would seem to come out of her, from her mouth and the pores of her skin.

Mrs. B. dreamt that she was skiing through the Arctic Ocean from Murmansk to the east. Her skis were skewed to the left, pulling her towards the open sea. The sun was setting behind her. She was searching for a friend who had left earlier. The glaciers sprang towards the sun like frozen fountains.

When she came to, the colours in the room were clearer, as if it had rained, and the sounds of the traffic from Acland Street. A feeling she had, of having to make some sort of irrevocable decision, passed over and lodged itself on the other side of a barrier, dividing her from the bright things of her world.

A client asked her one quiet afternoon, "Does this ever do anything to you, this business? Does it ever turn you on?"

Mrs B. shook her head.

"You're not like the others," he told her. "You're a funny one."

"You're the funny one." She smiled. "You can't imagine."

The client looked pleased. "I've always been an unconventional bloke."

"Jak sobie poscielisz tak sie wyspisz," said Mrs B. "In English it means, I think, 'You make your bed, then you better sleep in it'."

The client finished combing his hair and smoothed down his business suit. "I'm going away for a few weeks, but I'll come and see you when I get back." He left her a five dollar tip.

When Mrs B. began to sing, it was with the voice of a baby strangled at birth. It was impossible to listen to. It made ordinarily tough people cringe. If she forgot herself and started singing in the rooms, the hackles on the client's neck would rise. Tony, who wore the shirt with bravado, drew back at the sound of it and told her sharply she wasn't to sing when there were clients around.

It was the voice of a migrant, centuries old, who had kept travelling. At the end of the journey her mind carried her back and made her repeat it, inhabiting another body, or a memory without an anchor. The people she sang of no longer knew their place in the present, or, if they recognised it momentarily, it was quickly gone. It was the song of convict women, raped more times than it was worth remembering, seeds thrown by a strong arm from an old ship. She didn't think of them as she sang, but of her own personal history, running away from a European war. And the men, warming to her because her body never lost its ambiguous receptiveness, were shaken out of their calm, blasted by a voice that was a terrible bag-pipe of a joke.

There was one long weekend when the place was packed with interstate visitors and Denise was off sick. Mrs B. and the new girl did fifteen clients each in under three hours. Mrs B. fell into a chair and her legs were heavy. Inside she felt hollowed out, like a cave in a river bank that the next rains would fill to overflowing. Tony sat in the kitchen getting stoned, scarcely able to take in their success, wanting to hang on to something before the rush was over and the clients disappeared. Then he hit on it. Mrs B. would do a strip act.

"Me?" she said.

"But you'd be excellent," he told her. "Come on mate. Don't let me down now."

The phone rang and in her confusion Mrs B. picked up the receiver and put it down again without saying hello.

Tony raced out to buy things. Mrs B. felt as if the underground

river that was her insides was only just beginning to test its banks.
Tony came back with a sequinned bolero and stars for her nipples,
the way the strippers wore them up at the George, and a tasselled
G-string and various assorted small garments, some of which fitted
and some didn't. They impressed Mrs B. with the indelible fact of
their hardness and slipperiness.

Tony was trying out different songs, searching for something
that would fit. Mrs B. was trying to stop her hands from shaking. As
every second passed, she was on the verge of screaming, "Enough!"
Some strange hypnotic carry-over divided her mind from her body
the way it had in the rooms.

The clothes seemed to have a resistance of their own towards
being put on and taken off. Tony kept lighting joints for her, as if
the dope would make her a dancer. She tried to make do with a kind
of flounce of the top part of her body. The small hooks of the bolero
were invisible in the nest of sequins. Things kept sort of slipping out
of place and her breasts appeared too early. She seemed to have lost
control over them, as if, of their own accord, they had decided to get
it over quickly.

She was afraid of losing the things she had hidden behind, but at
the same time caught up in the glitter of herself, transfixed, almost,
by the reflection of the sequins, following the prismatic curve of her
neck into the mirror that Tony held up with a big smile of reassurance,
discovering, in the act of creating it, his faith in her.

She felt his smile slide along the surface of the river that was flowing so fast now there was no hope of stopping it. Her hands worked
on their own, taking their time, as if they had learnt the movements
of seduction in another life. Her mind played over the surface, not
even focused, as it had been in the rooms, on a table leg, a piece of
towel, the faded edge of a flower. Her mind wandered from bank to
bank and with the first whiff of the sea in her nostrils, taking her
chance when Tony left her for a moment, she danced out of the
room, her legs and arms taking charge at last. She flashed her sequins,
negotiating the corridor in a series of intricate and dainty steps, out
into the traffic of Acland Street.

# EILEEN SIMS

## A Victorian Frame of Mind

It was his interest in her collection of Victoriana that the old woman liked. He was so different from the other field officer who had been to see her. She revelled in his enthusiasm at the remnants of her bric-a-brac . . . the silver stand of the emu egg holder, so fine — surely a work of art. And the coffee set, so delicate. So unusual. It reminded him very much of one he had seen in an antique shop. The set was priced at $660. He fingered the cup.

He had just bought an Edwardian home in one of the inner suburbs. The house was close to the trams and the shops. She knew the district well. She had lived there before she married and had moved into this house. "There are many fine old homes there," she said.

"Yes, true, but not as many are large like this. The speculators are demolishing them."

"It is such a shame. Would you like more coffee?" She poured from the pot. "$660! If I really thought that this set was worth that much money, I wouldn't use it."

He lifted his cup. "It is very similar. Just think, this cup alone could be worth about $70!"

She noticed that her hand was shaking as she replaced the coffee pot on the tray. The set worth more than she had in the bank. One cup worth more than her weekly pension.

"This coffee set is really quite old. Someone gave it to my grandparents when they were married. They gave it to me for my twenty first birthday. I treasure it just for those reasons."

"All sentimental reasons."

"Yes. I've hardly used it. My late husband refused to drink from cups this size — 'Give me a man's cup of coffee', he'd say, 'not one of those thimble fool things'." She laughed. "Now I don't suppose I'll use it again. You tend to appreciate things more when you know their value." But she sounded doubtful.

"That is so right. Now take this house of yours, it would be worth a great deal of money at today's market prices."

She surprised him when he saw she was nodding her head in agreement. "I had the house valued last year. The rates went up . . ."

"But you would get the rate rebate," he said.

"Yes, I do, but the rates were really so high I went down to the Council and the young man there told me what the current market value of my house is. It's just unbelievable!"

"It is not unbelievable," he corrected.

"I suppose it is inflation rising all the time."

"You don't have to tell me about inflation. I suffer from it too."

"But each week prices go up . . . bread . . . now it's . . ."

"Last night I paid five dollars for a piece of grilling steak," he said.

She laughed. "Wait till you're my age. You won't be able to eat grilling steak which is just as well as I couldn't afford it at that price. I like a nice knuckle stew or neck chops, even a pound of mince steak."

"You mean five hundred grams."

"Oh dear, do I? These metric measures and weights . . . I'm at a loss. I think that at my old age I could be excused from even pretending to learn them. What's the point in trying to change things. And just what *is* a kilogram?"

"Well," he was smiling. "Put it this way. If you were living with someone, you would need to buy a kilogram."

He watched her drink her coffee. She did not speak, so he looked around the room again. The late afternoon sun was barely penetrating the blue glass of the leadlight window, but the pink glass was rosy and seemed to highlight the red glass of an oil lamp on a nearby table. It had been an elegant room in its day. He looked at the ceiling rose. The reproductions were not the same, despite what the makers claimed. But overall, it was a cold house. He looked at the fireplace. "I expect that has a good draw?"

She followed the direction in which he was looking. "The fireplace? I don't use it now. An open fire like that is too dangerous for me. I've had some accidents with falling logs from the grate and sparks too, flying out onto the carpet. I can't move quickly enough. Besides, I can't chop the wood."

"What you need is someone to chop the wood for you."

"I use that these days." She pointed to a kerosene heater.

"Haven't you got a man around the place who could chop the wood for you?"

"The heater is good enough."

He shivered and picked up the clipboard he had put down beside him while having his coffee. He remembered what the supervisor had said to them in the training sessions. "You can get people to tell you all kinds of things when you go to interview them. Each field officer will develop his own style of work. You can share a cup of tea with a person and act like their friend. It's what all the welfare people call 'empathy'."

They had all laughed. The supervisor had continued: "That's just a fancy word for getting on side. The other thing to learn is to observe. Use your eyes effectively. A good field officer can observe a multitude between the front door and the kitchen. As you walk down the passage, look into the rooms as you pass. The law doesn't actually allow us to search people's houses, but if they won't let you in, then I say they have something to hide."

When he had followed the old woman down the passage and into this room, he had observed. He had looked into the rooms as they passed. He had seen a man's clothing draped over the back of a chair.

"Don't you know a man who would chop wood for you?"

"Wood is too expensive. I can't afford it on the pension." She lifted the coffee pot. "I can't offer you any more coffee. The pot is empty."

He sighed. He was sure that she was hiding something from him. He knew there was a man living in the house. He sniffed the air. The house was musty, but there was also another smell, sweet. Tobacco. It was tobacco. Holding back his excitement, he said: "What's that aroma? It's this wood, isn't it?" He leaned forward and rubbed his hand against the table. "Cedar. There is nothing quite like it."

He noticed how she had turned quickly away from him towards the chiffonier that stood against the wall. As she stood, so did he and he reached the piece of furniture before she did. He looked for the pipe and the tobacco.

"It's this." She lifted a large bowl filled with dried flowers and buds. "Smell it," and she held it under his nose. "Mother always kept at least one big bowl of pot pourri in the house and I do too. These are all flowers from my own garden."

"Ah yes, all the flowers from these lovely old gardens — roses, lavender, rosemary . . ."

"You like old gardens, too? Well, come and see mine."

"But it's getting late . . . " She was walking from him.

"It's such a large garden. It is too much for me to manage by myself."

He followed her. Through the kitchen — old fashioned, a wooden sink (good God, did they still exist?), through the lean-to back porch with the wicker chairs around the small table. There on the table was a man's hat. He almost tripped over her to see into the back garden.

The yard stretched in front of him. This alone was large enough for a block of flats. But the garden itself was a mess. A climbing rose and honeysuckle fought for survival over a slanting trellis. Weeds stood in some places as high as the unkempt garden shrubs. The apple trees still held rotting fruit from the last season.

And then he saw what he was looking for. A cleared patch, recently turned and the pitchfork still propped in the soil.

She was saying: "It is too much for me to do."

"Well, who did this?" His voice was brusque with excited anticipation. Now he had the old girl. It was like the supervisor had said. You do get a sort of smell for deception.

The woman was blushing. "He's a very good friend."

"Very good friend, eh?"

"He likes to garden."

"And to live here, too?" He regretted saying it straight out like that, but it was too late now.

"How dare you say that!"

"Well, that's his hat in there on the table, isn't it?"

She turned and walked briskly back towards the house. He followed and liked hearing the sound of his footsteps clacking on the verandah tiles.

"And there's that men's clothing over there, in that room across the passage." She looked at him sharply. "Draped over the back of the chair. I saw it."

"That room was my late husband's." She paused. "Yes, there is clothing in there, but it is my husband's clothing. I put it there so . . . so I don't feel so lonely."

He laughed, but heard only his laughter echoing through the hollowness in the house. She led the way to the room. "Do men wear clothes like this today?" She held up pants with broad white braces, a collarless shirt and a beige cotton jacket. "Well, do they?"

she demanded.

He could tell that she was angry. He would try to get around her again. But before he could say anything, she was thrusting her finger onto his chest. "You think I'm living with a man, don't you?"

"No . . . yes . . . well . . . " he flustered.

"I could report you to the Ombudsman for defamation of character and harrassment."

He had failed. What would the supervisor say? He tried to smile. "It's all a part of the job. I'm sorry, but we meet them every day . . . people who are trying to cheat the government."

"Please go," she said.

He heard the tiredness in her voice. He would empathise.

"Look, I know this clothing of your husband's means a lot to you, reminding you of him and all that. But I know a dealer who would pay a packet for old clothes like this."

As he left the house, he thought he should say something else. He certainly did not want the Ombudsman involved. But he didn't know what else to say. So he stared at her sternly. It was then that he observed that she was crying.

As he heard the door close, he shrugged. Well, at least nobody could say he didn't try.

# ALISON TILSON

## Justice

Early morning and the boat pulls in. It is dark. It is cold. Street lights are fading yellow zones. A pale blue light appears behind the houses, turns slightly pink and yellow, and then there is sunlight. The houses take on dimension and colour. Solid cloud fills most of the sky. The sunlight is thin. The air seems grey. The clouds move quickly. A strong cold wind hits the skin and blows skirts, hats and cardigans about. People pull scarves and lapels across their chests and walk with their shoulders hunched. Hair blows against faces and into people's eyes.

A man's cap lifts and is carried over the edge of the dock into the water. It floats a moment, then disappears in shadow.

The pier seems very long. Wind pushes against the body and makes it difficult to walk. Words disappear, even when shouted. The wind blows into an open mouth and scrapes the back of the throat. It is easier not to talk. Just keep walking.

Maria's husband walks beside her and carries her bag. He gestures to her to hurry up.

———————

("My husband, my husband, where are you now, my brave strong husband, my brown strong husband with fierce dark eyes. My husband by whom I have been with child. Where are you now my brave strong husband? My husband who has written sending money for fares, my husband who has waited from far away. My husband in a land where no one is poor. I wait for your body and the sound of your voice.

Together we will work, now as husband and wife, together in a new land we will make a home for our children.")

---

In the village the marriage was not good. Maria wished to return to her mother.

"You must do more work," the father-in-law would say.

"Out of my kitchen. Leave that alone." The mother-in-law said. Her husband worked in the hills all day.

In the village, a woman much disliked or feared is said to be a witch.

Maria wished to return to the house of her mother and take with her the baby, the son of the husband.

"She is not a proper wife," the sister-in-law said.

"She is a wicked woman," the mother-in-law said.

"Her mother casts spells to call her back," the mother-in-law said. "Her mother is a witch."

"They are both of them the same," the sister-in-law said. "Bad women both of them."

"A curse on our house," the mother-in-law said.

"Only a bad woman would leave her husband and take with her his son."

The rumour is out. Maria Sevlovia is known to be a witch. Mothers beware. Children stay away. Keep a close watch and do nothing to incite.

She is not fit to bear children. She is not fit to raise a child. Georgio, the child. We must protect him from her wickedness.

---

Wanted Machinists Finishers Hemmers. Wanted. Machinists Finishers. Also Juniors to learn. Wanted. Machinists Finishers Hemmers. Apply fourth floor. Vacancies Machinists. Machinists experienced. For Frocks and Shirts. Apply Gilmore and Spicer 6th floor 175. Sonnies Second floor in Flinders Lane Vacancies Machinists. Sample hand wanted. Apply first floor. Wanted Machinists Finishers Hemmers. Wanted Machinists. Apply first floor.

---

Maria works hard. She stitches and sews. Maria is pleased to be in the new country. Maria and her husband are buying a house. Maria is pregnant. And only four months she has been working in Australia. Who will look after the child? Maria is pregnant. But the money. The money is needed.

Maria's husband sends for his mother and sister. Maria is pregnant. There will be two children. The son, Georgio, four years old and growing up in the village and now this new child soon to be born. Georgio will come to Australia with his grandmother and aunt. There will be soon a whole family. Maria's husband sends the money. Maria continues to work. The money is needed.

---

Two weeks they have all been living in the new house together.

"A witch. A witch. She is a witch. My son has married for a wife a witch."

The mother-in-law laments, throwing up her arms and walking the kitchen, back and forth.

"Keep her away from the food. She will poison my son."

"She must not touch the food," the sister-in-law agrees.

The cupboards are bolted. The fridge is chained with a padlock from its door.

Each evening Maria is served a meal cooked by her sister-in-law. Maria eats alone. Maria is forbidden to enter the kitchen.

Each morning Maria rises at 10 past 6. Six days of the week Maria works. She prepares herself and leaves for the fifteen minute walk to the 7 o'clock bus. Maria Sevlovia is never late. The bus rattles and shakes its way down Footscray Road. Each Friday she hands her pay packet to her husband. He counts it carefully and returns $5.40 to her — the exact amount for six days' fares.

On the seventh day Maria rises at 6am. She goes to Mass. She is expected to spend the day washing and ironing the family's clothes and tending the garden. She must dig the garden, weed the garden, water the garden and stake the plants. But always the mother-in-law watches lest a spell is cast on the plants.

On Sunday evening there is the television to be watched. Maria is allowed to join the family but is required to sit in a particular chair. She hand stitches clothes while the television provides a kaleidescope of pictures and a cacophony of sound. No one speaks English to follow the story.

---

Maria is forbidden to feed her son. Maria is forbidden to hold her son. Maria is forbidden to play with her son. Maria has in her purse one photograph of her son. Each morning, when she finds a seat on the bus, she opens her purse and looks at the photo. She does not speak to the other passengers.

---

It is the women working the service of the master. Who is it makes these systems of woman against woman, mother against mother, mother against child? Who is it benefits from such dislocation? The women are working the service of the master.

---

Maria clocks on to work at 12.15pm after the lunch break. At 2.09 the contractions begin. She goes into labour on the factory floor. By 4pm the baby has been born. Maria's husband visits her in the hospital once. Two months after the child is born Maria is back at work.

"The money, the money," her husband says.

---

The first blow is with an open hand. The swing is wide. The arm comes from behind the shoulder, a wide arc, the elbow bends at the last moment. The hand connects with Maria across her left cheek.

It is her stupidity again. Last time she had fallen asleep leaving a bed lamp on longer than is necessary. One time it was her hair cut.

Another time a glass of ouzo she had knocked over. Once he had accused her of talking to another man.

She has left the hose turned on in the garden longer than is necessary for the newly planted seedlings.

The second blow lands across her ear. Maria closes her eyes. The husband takes this opportunity to hit her mouth. Then twice her jaw. The sister-in-law and mother-in-law watch from the corner of the servery of the new kitchen. He grabs her left shoulder with his right hand and her right shoulder with his left hand and he shakes her vigorously. Maria's eyes are closed tight. She is frowning. The words he uses are loud and not pretty. He throws her across the room and she stumbles and falls on the arm of the couch.

Maria's husband swears loudly. There is a slight pause.

"Remember her powers," the mother-in-law warns.

Maria's husband follows Maria, pulls her up from the couch and punches her several times, using both hands, to the face and body.

Maria's eye is swollen. Her nose is bleeding. Her bottom lip is split and blood covers her teeth. Tomorrow she will notice two large bruises on her rib cage. Her stomach is aching. She falls to the floor. He kicks twice into her stomach, around which she is protectively curled. He stands over her. His chest is heaving. He stands above her waiting for his breathing to slow. His breathing slows.

"Get to your room," he says. His arms are on his hips.

"Bring me my dinner," he shouts to the women in the kitchen as he wipes his hands on a dress that is drying and crosses the room to sit at the dining table. The sister goes to the pot that is boiling on the stove and the mother holds the plate.

———

Maria Sevlovia leaves her husband. She takes her two children and goes to stay with a friend who lives alone. Maria's husband comes one afternoon and steals back their son. Maria keeps the last born child, a girl.

———

Pre-Trial Hearing:
The Family Court decides what will happen to the two children.

Care and Control:

The two children are to live with Maria.

Access:

The husband is to have the children every second weekend from 10am Saturday until 5pm Sunday, and for half of every school holiday.

———————

10am Saturday morning and the car pulls up outside Maria's house. He parks behind the bushes. Maria sees him coming up the path. She opens the door and pushes Georgio on to the verandah.

"Go to your father," she says. "Go. Go."

Maria runs inside and locks the door.

"Poppa," Georgio says.

"Georgio. Come see what Poppa's got for you. Where is Marianna?" the father says.

"Inside," Georgio says.

"Huh?" the father says and bangs on the door. "Maria. It's me. I've come for the children. Hurry up," he shouts. Maria crouches behind the door.

"You can't have Marianna," Maria says.

"Don't be stupid, woman. I've come for the children. Open the door." He leans on the door.

"You can't have Marianna. Take Georgio. Your son is enough. Tell him lies. Lies all day, lies all night. 'Your mother is a witch. Your mother is a bad bad woman.' Tell him lies. But you won't take Marianna. Marianna stays with me." Maria is shouting and tears are running down her face. Her husband begins to punch and kick the door.

"Lies, lies. I'll give you lies," he screams again and again. "Give me my daughter."

Georgio begins to cry.

"Go to the car Georgio."

"Poppa, Poppa." Georgio is crying and pulling at his father's trouser leg.

Maria is crouched a few feet from the door with a vase in her hand.

"Marianna is not here," she yells. "I've sent her away."

"Poppa Poppa," Georgio cries.

"What did you say, you stupid woman?" her husband yells. He stops pounding the door.

"I've sent her away. She's not here," Maria says.

"Georgio, where is Marianna?"

"Poppa Poppa," Georgio screams. "Poppa Poppa."

Maria's husband curses violently and gives the door one solid kick before he leaves carrying Georgio in his arms.

"Bad. Bad. Your mother is a bad woman, Georgio."

"You are a curse on our children," the husband screams as the gate slams.

"Bad. Bad." Georgio cries. "Bad. Bad."

Maria runs into the kitchen. She falls to a chair and sobs with her hands to her face.

———————

The walls are wood panelled. One wall is all windows. The solicitor sits behind a large wooden desk. Files and papers are heaped on top of it. The solicitor pushes a button and says,

"Miss Wilson. I have a client with me. Please hold all calls." He looks up.

"Mrs Sevlovia. Your husband alleges that you have refused to allow him access to his daughter on five occasions. I have here a document seeking to have you dealt with for contempt of the orders of the court. Do you realise the severity of this situation?"

Maria says nothing.

"It is my obligation to inform you that you can be imprisoned for these instances of contempt." He looks up.

Maria says nothing.

"I am referring to your refusal to allow your husband access to both his children. Is it correct that you did on these dates refuse to deliver Marianna to your husband?"

Maria says nothing.

"These court orders must be obeyed, Mrs Sevlovia. Do you under- stand that?"

"He cannot have my daughter," Maria says. "I will go to jail, but he cannot have my daughter."

"Mrs Sevlovia, the court has ordered that your husband be given access to both children every second weekend between the hours of ..."

"No. No. He cannot have my daughter. To fill her head with lies. No. He cannot have her."

"Let me make myself clear, Mrs Sevlovia." The solicitor leans forward. "Unless you obey these orders you will be penalised. Interim Care and Control is at present awarded to you. But if you continue to disregard these access orders Care and Control may be awarded to your husband. The Commonwealth Police may be called in. You may go to jail. Do I make myself clear? You must obey these orders."

"He cannot have my daughter. I will go to jail."

"If you go to jail, Mrs Sevlovia, who will care for your children?" Maria says nothing.

The solicitor leans back.

"Now then. Let us prepare our defence."

---

1.  Bourke Street is tree-lined between William and King Streets.
2.  Number 570 Bourke is a white, many-windowed, sky scraper with a plaza. There are cubes of modern sculpture on the plaza.
3.  Inside the building, on the south of the ground floor is an Ansett Airlines travel office, and on the north, the CBA bank. At the centre and back of the floor are blocks of lifts.
4.  Lifts to the Family Court are in the row against the back wall.
5.  The Family Court is on the 17th floor.
    The lift travels express to the 17th floor.
6.  FAMILY COURT OF AUSTRALIA.
    All persons to report to Court Reception at other end of lobby.
7.  Private. No Admittance; Court 1; Waiting 5; No Smoking; Family Court Counsellor 11; Court Reporters; Family Court Counsellor 12; Waiting 4; Court 2; Closed Court in Session; Private. No Admittance.
8.  The chairs are lime green plastic. People wait in a row with their backs to the centre walls. There is a single indoor plant in a white plastic tub.
9.  Important men with straight backs and protruding bellies clutch folders to their chests.
10. TNT Security Guards walk briskly. Silver guns with wooden handles stick out of holsters.

---

Court 2. Closed Court in Session. Mrs Maria Sevlovia follows the solicitor and barrister into the court. She sits where the solicitor directs her, on a row of green chairs against the back wall. Her husband is already seated at the end of the row. When she comes in, he turns his body away from her, sniffs and holds his head higher.

The Judge enters from a door at the far end of the room. Everyone stands up. He walks to the centre of the bench that extends almost the width of the room. He sits behind it, waits a moment and then looks up. Everyone bows. Everyone sits down.

"The matter of Sevlovia," the Orderly says loudly from his desk in front of the Judge's bench. Maria's husband's barrister stands, pushes his chair in, leans on the back of it and coughs slightly.

"Your Honour, I appear on behalf of the husband."

He sits.

Maria's barrister stands.

"If the Court pleases, I appear on behalf of the wife."

He sits.

Maria's husband's barrister adjusts the books and papers in front of him. It is a large wooden desk they all sit at. He stands again, takes up his position and begins.

"Your Honour, this is an application by the husband that the wife be dealt with for contempt of court. On the 6th day of March 1980 the court made orders, 1. that the wife have Care and Control of the children of the marriage, of Georgio and Marianna and, 2. that the husband should have access to the said children every second weekend from the hours of 10am Saturday until 5pm Sunday and half of all school holidays."

"Your Honour, in the husband's affidavit, sworn on the 18th day of June 1980, he sets out the occasions on which the wife has failed to comply with the orders of the court. June 14th, 1980. May 31st, 1980. May 17th, 1980. May 3rd, 1980. April 19th, 1980. That is, she failed to deliver the child, Marianna, to the husband for access on those days. On each of these occasions the wife was prepared to allow access to the son, Georgio, but refused to deliver the daughter, Marianna, to the husband."

"Your Honour, it is my submission that the time is now appropriate for the Court to make the necessary orders to enable the husband to have access to his child."

The barrister sits down.

Maria's barrister stands and begins.

"Your Honour, the wife has in the past had some difficulty in understanding the terms of the orders of the court. But she has agreed to comply in future with the orders and deliver both children to the husband for access every alternate weekend....."

Maria Sevlovia is standing up. Maria Sevlovia is speaking.

"He cannot have her. Marianna cannot go."

"Shsh," the barrister says, "Sit down."

"Quiet," the solicitor says, "Sit down, Mrs Sevlovia. Please."

Maria is speaking more loudly.

"It is my husband and the family, they make my daughter — "

The Orderly gesticulates. He is pointing at her. "Down, down," he mouthes.

"— against me. She cannot go." Maria Sevlovia is shouting. "I will not have it. She cannot go."

The Judge is looking at Maria's barrister.

"Mr Morrison, if you cannot quieten your client I shall be obliged to leave the bench."

Maria Sevlovia is shouting.

"She is my daughter. He cannot have my daughter. She cannot go. She cannot go."

The Judge leaves the bench.

Maria Sevlovia is shouting.

Two security guards come through the door.

---

The road is wide and straight. There is one set of traffic lights far away. Only the lines of light poles and lights stretch across the sky. There is uninterrupted sky above the road.

On one side a parkland, a pavilion, an oval. A line of trees at the edge of the road, very green, with many leaves, unlike the Australian gum, cut off by the council and branches with cut stubby ends. On the other side, houses and flats, a line of tidy buildings. Then parkland both sides, a very old bridge with steep sharp slopes to a creek perhaps. The road dips and turns. As it turns, some multi-storey housing commission flats, very tall, white, with many windows.

The car stops. Many cars pass on the left. Most have only one person in them, looking intently at the road. The car turns right through some traffic lights then down a small narrow road, like in the country. There are trees on both sides and meeting over the road. It is very bumpy. The car bounces.

A man is jogging down the side of the road. He wears a blue t-shirt and blue shorts. Two people on bikes ride past in the opposite direction and their faces cannot be seen. A man is walking an alsatian dog on a leash. There is parkland on both sides but down one side some buildings and a lot of wire-mesh fence.

The road winds right then left, then the car slows, turns suddenly left and stops. Doors open. There is noise and talking. Out the back window is the road and trees and green. The wind is in the trees and the sun glints against the edges of the leaves.

The car starts again and goes through two large white brick pillars. On top of a red brick building at one side, high in the air, are huge rolls of barbed wire.

A grey metal roller door begins to come down between the two white pillars and then we are inside.

# JANNETTE McKEMMISH

**The Spider Stories**

(i) A change in the weather.

The spider has been on the ceiling for five days now, counting today.

The rain began early in the morning. Quiet at first, a few practice drops to warn lazy ants and spiders inside. Settling in to steady rhythms, drumming the dawn through grey haze and half light, a watery day meets the (fading) night.

I've not seen the spider move yet although it changes places each day, achieving by leaps and jumps I'm sure, the piece of roof above my bed.

I didn't notice the spider at all when I woke up to pace the long hallway, stamping the cramp from thigh to calf to foot and out to the worn grey floral carpet. I guess I was too distracted by visions of varicose veins, blood clots, thrombosis, embolisms, heart attacks, blindness and all the other costs of contraception.

It is on the wall between the picture rail and roof, sideways, vertical.

The dream event climaxed with the noisy arrival of fire engines and tanks. Panic. Panic. The sirens sound on and on, driving to panic. The people disappear, dematerialise. The voice shouts, do something, save yourself. The alarm clock is shouting at my eyes to open. The

mind resists a moment then leaps into the day, urging arms to fly
out, meet the button. Nothing moves. The eyes are staring, a blurred
image of a high white ceiling defining a small brown furred mark
above my bed, above my head.

What do spiders see?

Snuggling in to the warmth of slept sheets, breathing the smell of
sweetened sweat, damp reminders of a night of love. I remember how
these sheets got soiled and sense that not even the precious way your
lips caress my thigh can convince me it is worth facing lone spiders
first thing in the morning.

I promise this spider death.

(ii) I wish there weren't three spiders on my roof today.

The small huntsman was OK. It's been around for days, keeping its
distance, even looking cute occasionally. But the extremely large,
enormously intimidating huntsman right above my desk as I write,
well, to be completely frank (direct and intense), I do wish it/he/she
wasn't there.

It wasn't there this morning when I awoke to see the sun rise on the
way to bathroom and breakfast . . .

When I got home this afternoon there was only the small one. Late
at night, with the deep darkness, came the large one. And then
another, in a separate corner. They dash about and take up different
poses when I leave the room to make tea. At night when I sleep they
gallop, I can almost hear them, their movement wakes me, I stare,
disbelieving, at their audacity.

It occurs to me at around four in the morning that the gargantuan
huntsman has probably been living in the room for as many years as I
have. I go into a frenzy of overdue packing. Books in boxes, bags of
discarded clothes and piles of old lesson plans and school teacher
paper warfare. I make mountains of possessions on the floor, I sort
and make decisions, read letters from people I've forgotten. By dawn I
have broken the back of the unattractive part of moving and retire

to an empty room down the hall. I sleep until mid-day and emerge rested, relaxed. The spiders have moved into the hall. All of them. They are looking for me, I mutter, as I dash through the doorway to a room now free from spiders.

I spend four more days in that house. Sleeping in any empty room. The spiders wander up and down the hallway, high on the walls. They pay visits to other people's rooms but I elude them by constant change. I depart feeling reasonably paranoid and mildly victorious.

(iii) I step off the train at the deserted railway station and walk across the bare paddock to meet my sister at the pub. I am incongruous in a fur coat with too many pieces of luggage. We chat on as we drive to her newly acquired farm house. It's only small, she says, but it has a lovely old garden. The old Franklin place, you remember it, with climbing roses and wisteria and passionfruit and peppercorn trees. I am immediately sorry it is dark. We pull into the driveway and approach the house. Ah. She says. I'd better warn you. That lovely trellis covered in vines is a bit of a ...um ...how should I put it? Well. See this broom here. Well. We use that to brush the tree-spider webs away. It doesn't make any difference. They make new webs each day. But at least you can get to the back door.

I think briefly of asking where the front door is and then am overcome with the image of being housebound for a week in the middle of a lovely garden. And they are sure to have an outside dunny.

> But here, where the spiders are epidemic, I am not the target.
> It is different.
> And then everything is different here.
> The spiders may be the least of it.

(iv) I am spider phobic.

I am spider phobic for very good reasons. They plague me. Consider:

The small black spider sits in the corner of my flat for days, perhaps even weeks. I am blase. I notice it occasionally but generally ignore it. I go to Helen's class and read chapter one to a group of students, men and women. The next morning as I am having breakfast in bed at eight o'clock in order to greet the Social Security man with a semblance of ordinariness, the spider drops, unnoticed from its corner and walks along my arm. Quite enough said.

Or consider this:
We pack up the cars between Christmas and New Year and head north for a week at the beach. All the regular camping grounds are full of course but we manage to find a superior paddock with toilets and a rubbish bin a mere ten yards from the surf. We set up the tents and have several wonderful days on the beach or under the paper bark and palm trees. Someone even sleeps outside. It is all very peaceful and healthy and without anxiety.

I crawl out of the tent at seven in the morning to find Virginia crouched and staring at the mattress and blanket that was Pat's bed. Don't panic, she says, but underneath that blanket, look, you can see it moving, is a large black furry spider.

Jesus. Say I. Kill it. You have to kill it. A voice calls from another tent, aroused by the hysterical tones of our normally relaxed voices. What is it? What does it look like? We pull the blanket back and the black monster makes a dash for Virginia. It is definitely a big black muscular furry spider. It's a funnel web, says the voice from the tent . . . . . . . . horror strikes my heart as I say in a low voice, very calmly, well, you'll just have to kill it Virginia. I can't bear it.

She kills it quite easily with a shoe. There is no fatal bite, no instant death. I rest my case nonetheless and maintain that that spider would not have been in that paddock if I had not been there too.

(v) I have no intention of tempting fate by writing the last spider story.

## The Influence of Public Transport on the Feminist Aesthetic

First Voice

absolutely

I know how you feel
I know you know how I feel
remember
four gins and that everyday tone
'I like travelling on buses alone.'

Home from work sixish, day light saving wide awake, cup of tea, just one biscuit, might as well have two, where is she?

The phone rings. It is our regular wrong number. Harbour Lightridge Company, pretty tugs on the water. If we are getting their calls they are getting ours, so the telecom lady tells me. I wish I were their receptionist to answer your call.

I take the phone off the hook after three raised hopes. None are for me sitting here by the phone smoking tailor-mades make the room stink sour for days. At nine it is dark and I go out walking, walking.

Saturday morning. It can't be eight o'clock and I can't be wide awake with nothing but domesticity. I could ring Di or Julie, go to the markets accompanied in the sun, turning all the pretty things to find a bargain or something I cannot live without. I cannot live without you.

Drinking in the pub, dark and grimy corners, bright beach weather outside, taking existential pride over such despair. So studied it shows as addiction to the style, waiting for the Space Invaders machine, slurring jokes that aren't funny if you are sober, abandoning sense to another packet of smokes.

I used to say she was the best thing about me until she wasn't around, and I couldn't. Say anything. Say anything I whispered into the phone silence. Just speak. That isn't too much to ask. Don't I have a right to something.

She tells me a funny story to make humiliation complete.

What have you been doing.

Mourning.

Who died?

I did.

At least you will have good copy — the lady writer driven to despair. Fuck. You know what I think about therapeutic art and negativity's not my subject. I've been crying in the hope that someone might hear, take pity. But I cannot bear the visitors with gossip and good intentions. I want you.

Remember when we said all that stuff about gossip: stylised, up front, stripped of its malice. Right now it doesn't amuse. There is no pleasure in knowing that this absolute commands a good price. I am furious with myself, the misery, how are you?

Fine, relieved. Freed. Sad too of course.

Perfunctory sorrow. Do you think I am enviable with my powerful emotions? I might go home to mother where no-one knows that women have bleeding hearts, or cares. A prodigal daughter holding it in, sipping whisky in a single bed, listening to the crickets and cicadas and the coughing through the wall. I won't cry there. Distance distances. Pain hurts. Did we handcuff each other to the still photograph of our last night together?

I have walked to your house every night this week. Standing in the shadows watching all the lights go out I smoke cigarettes and suppose that finally Woody Allen feels better than I do. When I am sure you are asleep I walk home, scared, sweating, though now it is winter and the lurking men are not so much around. The cars are frosty noises and I keep walking, striding, promising not to do the doubly dangerous thing again. Tonight I watched the late late movie, sobering up after falling about on the dance floor. Making sure I couldn't make it home alone. Making sure I would. At five a.m. I wander out the door, just to take a look at the dawn I tell myself, find a high point in this hilly city, the feet are round about your street, the shadows go and I feel silly, sober, silly, exposed to the waking people. It has been months. Maybe you don't even live there. I wait in the cafe on the corner, positioned with a watery capuccino, a view of all directions, eventually you will have to go by and I will see . . . . just a profile in an unfamiliar car. I am on foot and cannot track the mystery.

*  *  *  *

Second Voice

In the pub she dances completely out of time to the music which is slow and easy. Is she that drunk? That removed? A parody? An actress? She sways in a circle, feet fixed to an invisible spot, to safety. She threatens to topple, stumble, crumble publicly. She leans precarious and can't help helping herself. It is alright. I think she is not without control or pride. She does not demand my disgust.

Of course it couldn't last. Ran into her at the meeting on Wednesday night. She made a late entrance: trembling smile as heads turned and turned quickly away, as she knew they would. I nodded, trembled my own smile, I won't be the ogre, allow her the martyr. She spoke not a word or none above a whisper, but she had wan smiles for jokes and three cans of Carlton Draught, getting drunk quickly, she slipped out mere seconds before the meeting broke into brief socialising. Not out of control, I thought, a social stager still.

But when I got home there was the car and a silhouette leaning back in the front seat smoking, barely moving, her very own vigil. Creep. Jesus. Now who's the oppressor I muttered having had the odd can of beer myself. But I spoke softly and didn't point her out to Kath and later on, when the frost came down and I was making an insomniacal cup of tea, I took one out to her and we drove around, spilling tea on the dashboard and letting the heater thaw her out. That was a touching gesture on my part don't you think, but it was totally private, perhaps even she recalled it as a mad dream for I made her drive me home as soon as she was warmed, I slipped out and inside as soon as the car pulled up.

She had gone when I went off to work. The next afternoon I made sure there there were no spare car parks in the narrow street, stayed elsewhere for a few nights to stop myself from a second moment of relenting. Kath told me she saw her there on Friday night and, being Kath and antagonistic after all this she had a shout about her driving me further away, making an absolute fool of herself, credibility etc. I am sure it made Kath feel a lot better.

Got a note on Sunday:
>     hate and love are mutually defined
>     each other's other half
>     dependent
perhaps when you say you hate me
>     to my face
>     I will be close to happy
>     redundant.

Di was over so I showed it to her, asked advice. She wanted to know all the details but I couldn't . . . remember . . . retell . . . said, I am more bored than angry, have to protect myself. Di said I should return the notes unread, but even that is a response, and dangerous.

Carole harassed me a few days later about how badly I behaved, what had happened to my personal politics, lots of people were pretty pissed off about my ruthlessness, refusal to discuss. The age old feminist weapon, rhetoric, endless words, I refuse to collaborate. She is colourfully, pitiably insane, I am dully so.

October nearly wore me down with its winds and high racing clouds. Had to stay in bed for a couple of days, paralysed, terrified that she would find me weakened, susceptible to kindness. I would make thermoses of tea and go without food, sleeping, almost weeping when the dreams surfaced in ordinary guises, all my childhood crimes revisited, reinforcing this siege.

She has left me alone for a week. No tears. No difficult phone calls at one in the morning. No notes under the door, relentless over breakfast. I suspect she has gone away and start going about the town, relieved, freed, as I said to her, religiously, every day on the phone last week, it is over, leave me alone. She has left me alone. I am no longer haunted by the begging, the prostration that hurts because it is reminiscent. I have been like that. Knowing the depths and crevices of that I despise her more. How could I have loved her. She is our failure breathing weeping wanting haunting. Kath called it embarrassing, she said 'Oh dear, it must be so embarrassing for you.' And for her, I said, and for all of us.

* * * *

First Voice

On the train north I am smiling, an orgy of dual fantasies of spewing all the sadness and anger over the long-time friends, having them sit up with me late at night listening, writing the long letters of clever pleading, there's nowhere else to go but up and aren't you impressed with this diligent pain? Worn down by this excruciating refusal to accept?

The train is late and I haven't slept for a year. In the country the oxygen goes straight to the brain, wiping the crucial memory, perhaps it just surrendered to the cliches about time.

I have to look back at my diary, to that last page ever written. At the time I never believed it would be meant. I wrote:

> Anne was very quiet all weekend, that seething silence, the silence of absolutism, no hope. At lunch on Sunday we both sank into the day-before-Monday blues and I went accidentally to sleep, sprawled on the floor while the T.V. filled our lives. Desperately. She woke me roughly, shaking, wake up wake up, I want to tell you something . . . I can't bear this anymore. You must go. You are killing me. I am shaking my head and splashing water on my face, looking in the mirror for signs of the disease, what? What is it? What has happened?
>
> No, she says, No. No. You are not going to drag up another conversation. No verbal reconciliation. I've been knowing it for days, for as long as I can remember. You have to go. I don't want to talk about it. It is over. That is all.

In the country, seated in the chair in the sun, the diary mocks me. My life stopped with your words. A dramatic gesture perhaps. And I am appalled at the failure to record this passion, this case-study of extremism. It is gone, like all the hours of all the days spent without you, without myself . . . able only to let the sun seep through to the bones, believing in nothing, seeing nothing, paralysed by the friends and their distance, impatience. I stay up in the nights listening listening, sipping whisky in a single bed, sleeping at seven, awake after noon to accusing eyes, disappointment. Unfortunately I couldn't cry. In the end they asked me to leave, draining, invading their home with my grief, they said.

At Lismore I sent you a telegram 'arriving 9.30 Tues Central' as though I were an old friend visiting.

The platform was crowded without you and I wait on the seat under the high roof going blind with watching for your face. At eleven 'The Age' comes in and I read it all, news comics births deaths crossword. Eventually. One day. You will have to speak. Gesture toward me. Nod. Perhaps a smile and perhaps then, or soon after, I will turn to you and say yes, and hear the tables turned.

I catch the bus to your house never allowing that you might not be there. In this patient madness some moments must ring true. You answer the door, standing, unaffected, you expected . . . . Staring past my shoulder you make me ask if I can come in and I make you say no.

*     *     *     *

Second Voice

I turn and walk down the passage. She swings her pack to the floor, I hear the thump, she follows me into the kitchen. Other people are making a mess with the cappuccino machine, they offer her coffee, she accepts, a crucial mistake.

I wander on into the backyard and politeness prevents her from following. The coffee takes forever and I sit on the garden wall. No tears. No words. She picks up my hand and speaks my name. Weariness erupts into incongruity, farce. She shakes her head, shudders. I laugh. She says "I am totally obsessed with the power of the C.I.A. There is nothing we can do any more, about anything."

When she left, I was glad she couldn't speak. Clearly I hate her but I said I would meet her for coffee tomorrow. Cannot care. Heard the news at six, an old habit of hers I haven't relinquished. A woman hit by a bus in George Street, holding up the peak hour traffic heading south along Broadway. Mentally noted to go to the Cross via Redfern.

Later on, when the dead woman's name was released, I said it should have been a truck. The buses, after all, are public transport and as such beyond our anger. She hated trucks and might have made her death a protest against their rampage through our streets.

# SAL BRERETON

## Ideal Conditions

At work I show an outward interest in the books & arrange them according to size & colour or in relation to each other's titles which leads to a logic they never seem to notice (of a deliberate try at commenting on the capitalist system) & which proves 'right' as the day wears on.

I come to see how I will 'use' these things — the light French muzak, the man who comes to the counter on Thursday night who smells of a brand of bath-soap, who obtains a large book from the 'Australiana' section & so on.

\* \* \*

"The way writing, independent of style or attitude or intentions, comes back to the writer's own knowledge of the situation of its being written. Not things you can prove 'true' or not, so much as the kind of thinking that goes with it."

I think about this in relation to some books on the desk. They're books by Australian male writers & a lot of them are presented inside a context that 'sounds' convincing & yet rarely is, either as idea or as sentiment. & they incorporate a subtle kind of sexism, or a more open 'ignorant' kind. I think if these writers are so easily able to ignore these issues, how 'available' is writing these days as a means of effecting any unconscious 'awareness' of one's attitudes.

\* \* \*

I recall coming into K.L. airport just before a storm. There were a lot of palm-trees. It struck me first how the Asians looked smaller in real life in this place — in white T-shirts & thongs in the heat.

This afternoon it reminds me of afternoon replays of Four Corners. I remember then I was thinking it too. It felt 'free' to be speeding down the freeway in a bus beside millions of scooters all racing to the city.

*        *        *

Lantana breaks the view up like memories of Bangkok everytime a Boeing comes over across the window & moves off & then I forget about tourism & look at the book I'm reading about Marxism. The front-page of the Herald is running an article on drugs & I think if it's 'uncontrollable' at first now the choice is here I'll believe in it for different reasons & even more 'effectively'. I think how business trips are often better than just 'going' O.S. I read this & later glue a recent postcard (from Micky) to the wall which is really an 'idea' that's become a habit & later a small bi-plane goes over like a vote of confidence.

*        *        *

Halfway between 'automatic' & feeling too affected by the circumstances to move freely, I end up spending hours in Wollongong in the cafe at David Jones. In the oval, two soccer teams do laps in yellow guernseys. I spend lunch-time looking for a white shirt. "Life illustrates, & the view illustrates something else" & when I get up to go, I see Tony Bond, director of the Art Gallery, taking a promising local sculptor to lunch.

*        *        *

*Day off*

Today Monday, the only day 'off' in the week when I ever feel I'll sit down & write. I am reading the title poem of Pat Nolan's book that came Wednesday. In front on the window a few dandelions are drying out. The frames of the window throw bands of shadow on the table & move over it, & over the page I'm up to, in a slow, noticeable way that makes the whole tenor of the words more depressing. It's 9 o'clock. The trucks are running & the trains have been running for hours. In here, a blowfly hits itself on the window & flies round until

I get up, open the window & throw it out. Yesterday's dead snake is draped on the Mulberry tree. Beyond it, the ocean & the waves & above them two round clouds like a kite & zeppelin are just sitting there.

\* \* \*

I feel exhausted by Jane's manner. Bert Newton on the cover of Fatty Finn.

\* \* \*

I'm looking down the beach. It looks beautiful & in a way I think 'Nouveau Roman' before I think 'beautiful', & then I understand I began acknowledging things as beautiful this way.

\* \* \*

### My first taste of Structuralism

You'll discover you'll want to itemise everything, labels on boxes — anything that's written & visual, & that it all 'fits in' as well. I decide on getting up, leaving this & eating lunch. On the way, one of the cardboard boxes in the corner says: Berger: Keep on Keeping on. Today for a while (on the way inside) it makes the day seem worthwhile devoting to writing down the rest of them.

Inside I get a tin of Zanae Vine leaves, a carton of Cottage cheese, some Sockeye Salmon & balm tea & read the Herald in front of the heater. In front of it, I feel similarly 'drawn' to the room, though differently, & not descriptively. To name nouns & the way they're ordered would seem different from it, or too much like work or too static. Over lunch I discover it can be ideal, the way the room will just 'exist' as this separate still-life.

\* \* \*

Doing that seemed like one way to avoid a motivation to write based on a desire to let the act of 'writing' itself, rather than understanding, supply 'answers', or solve the feelings of doubt I had. I agreed with Adrienne Rich's statement that in an environment where language & naming are power, silence is oppression. It didn't seem useful though to *just* begin to write, & it had to involve a certain kind of 'honesty' as well.\*

*Eventually it *was* partly the act of writing itself that defended me against the feelings of inactivity I had, & against the continual outside events I found annoying & yet couldn't adequately locate or name.

* * *

Only 2 days to go.

Flags flying at Boyded in North Wollongong.

Narelle's boyfriend sells a Datsun &, at work, Narelle's hand restores my faith in palmistry.

* * *

It gives me a framework where I feel I can include anything — like this explanation. & it means not being limited by an attitude of certain 'forms' of writing — where things can be arranged to either 'look' or 'sound' convincing.

6.30 Right up, the sound of a large Boeing going over. I associate the noise with the introduction of daylight saving now & never Thailand.

In the way that I'd seen the diaries as passive & defensive (& in that way, limiting & false) I also started to see all other kinds of literary writing. I went through different forms of not-writing, a whole range of reasons or actions that were responsible for not-writing & not wanting to.

* * *

The force of it, like the force of anything 'in the present', & the choice of its meaning, approaches me like paranoia — not just threatening but useful — & as a vehicle not to be false in starting writing.

* * *

Often it feels like writers are using a poem or piece of writing to display a 'set' of responses or insights, & to 'confirm' them to themselves or socially. I would say this often occurs say, in a type of male 'diary', which makes use of the idea of 'privacy' as something to 'convince' themselves they *couldn't* possibly be doing this.

* * *

I get home & assume the events are somehow replaceable by a condition for writing, or by these problems of how to approach them. & eventually, over weeks, that becomes what's going on — knowing what I'm generally meant to be doing, & never sure what to expect next.

& it's difficult — the way the observations of the process become one, become the way themselves.

\* \* \*

Stoned, this morning, writing a letter to Alexandra in the room overlooking the coast, in the rain I hallucinate my hand's a horse on which I've just ridden into the set of a Western. My horse the size of a hand, & the buildings in the street, which are really words, are tiny ones. It triggers a memory of a street in Thailand. In it it's hot & I become more interested in this memory, than the hallucination or the act of writing.

Later, raining, in front of me on the calendar I observe the sun rising 7 minutes later a week as we head into winter. This feels interesting & then also visual like hallucination & 'like' a stretch of time.

# JERI KROLL

## Maslins Beach at Midnight

### January, 1981

One or two steps and we were in the dark. The water black as dye, as unbelievable hair. It brushed our ankles. Cool./No wind, so the moon kept from us, trapped above the clouds. Sand, flat as the end of the world. Midnight desert sheen. We could fall off if we waded out, the waves whispered. So we stood knee deep, washing off summer sweat, fresh as twilight. And wondered how people could exist/and where/since we were the only ones here/the only ones. Then the sea came alive. Pinpoints of light swelled far out, eddied near, splashed our knees. We knelt. Quicksilver coated our hands/we swirled water over our bodies/and rose, glistening sea creatures, phosphorescent as moon's own waves, as random as gods, as whole as the moment we first stepped into the dark.

## Falling Out

I hope that you thought of this assignment as if it were a matter of life and death for you, not just an intellectual game. You had to pick one aspect of shelter life, and to find one way of coping with it. Right. Now who's first?

Yes, Trudi, the population. Yes, that's a valid point to consider. No, I can't say that I'd thought of what effect IUDs would have with no doctors left to remove them. That would keep down mutations anyway, eh?

Doug. Water supplies severely limited. Chewing gum to keep the juices flowing? Think again, mate. We'll come back to you later, so you'd better be prepared next time round.

Christie. Yes, well, I know a dog would keep morale up, but think of all the valuable air, water and food it would consume. Protection against intruders? Well, yes, but if you've selected a properly secluded spot, you'd minimise the danger of unwelcome entry. Guns and ammunition would, no doubt, be part of the survival store. Oh, a pacifist. But you think it would be all right for your dog to tear your enemy limb from limb? And have you thought that you could always eat him in a pinch? No, look, I'm sorry. Don't get upset, I didn't know you'd just lost your dog.

Ah, yes, Wayne, crucial point. Food. Everyone's steered clear of that so far. Fresh meat and veg, definitely out. Canned food — space problem. Dehydrated food — water problem. So. . . . . . . .ah. Fasting practice. Yes, I've read Kafka's *The Hunger Artist*. But he finally died. And he had a vocation for it. Even yogis eat every once in a way. Bulk's necessary for proper functioning. Vitamins and laxatives? How long do you think you'd manage on those? You're only letting loose a flood of other problems: dehydration, disposal and so on.

OK. Now our footballer over there. Tim, what . . . ah, yes, it had occurred to me that this was a mixed company. What did you want to . . .? Well, of course we're all adults here. Sex is a necessity of sorts. Oh, the old Δ. I see. So what would you do? Three women and one man. A roster. With or without his consent? For the good of the community. Julie, yes, you can respond to . . . No, sit down. This is all theoretical, remember? It isn't? What goes on outside this room is — Janet, you have some amendment to make to Tim's proposal?

Reverse the situation: three men and one woman? More biologically sound, you say. Ha, ha, well now, that's certainly a debatable point. I mean, no I haven't read *The Hite Report*, but I do have a certain number of years of experience, but . . . now Rob, you've been nodding your head over there for quite a while. What's on your mind? Right, certainly if she became pregnant, for at least some of the time she'd be out of action, as you put it. But men have been known to fend for themselves in the past in times of crisis . . .

## Openings and Closings

### Two is Company (Pty Ltd)

She strode into his office, and slid a buttock onto the polished desk, nudging the calendar back. His eyelids flickered. Leaning over a fraction more, so that her bust cut off his desk light, she licked her dry lips, and stared point blank into his eyes.

### Accident

She slammed the car door, rustling the gum leaves overhead, which had been quiet all day until the waxed blue Commodore flowed back up the drive to its accustomed place. Inside, she knew he waited. So she stayed where she was.

### Last Call

The barman let down the wooden cage around himself, locking in the rainbow of bottles. Leslie still sat on the stool, kicking the front of the bar to the time of a half-remembered rock and roll song, about why birds sing, and lovers await the break of day. Fools. And she couldn't keep time with the motors gunning and the brakes screeching outside as the pub's clientele departed. She looked through the grill at the barman who was rinsing the last glasses. Then he wiped his hands on the T-shirt over his belly, lifted up the flap to the bar, turned and locked the last segment of the cage. His footsteps on the carpet sounded like beer slopping against a glass.

### Victim

Glenda crept up the carpeted stairs. She was so carefully balanced on the balls of her stockinged feet that she felt as if she were floating. She longed just once to slide down the bannister. As a child, she had never been allowed. But practised in silence and cunning since she could remember. And now, after all that had happened, here she was again in their house, keeping her own counsel, listening for voices. She stopped at the landing. Out the immaculate window, a pure moon hung above the jacaranda, now lush purple. Her eyes focused on the moon's surface. Wafer-thin some places; she could sense the dark on the other side. She knew what she had to do. So she left the moon above the trees, and quickly reached the top of the stairs.

# FINOLA MOORHEAD

## Novel in Ten Lines

Leone's room is not near the left bank of the river where she drowned. Harold walked by the parkbench, thinking. Thoughts of how & when & guilt were his and we are interested, also, in the clothes he wears, the trench coat with *Giovanni's Room* by James Baldwin in the pocket. Leone came from the country with blond hair that turned dark in the city – her cotton print dresses turned to brown pleated skirts. Leone was lonely. And Harold felt sorry, that's all. He had other friends, & lots of nights with other men: his own problems.

# Nun

The pregnant nun. The aborted nun. The frigid nun. The frustrated nun. The contented nun. The silent nun. The saintly nun. The mean nun. The proficient nun. The greedy nun. The secretive nun. The conservative nun. The radical nun. The inspired nun. The desired nun. The nun and the gardener. The nun and the priest. The nun and the monk. The nun and the altar boy. The nun and the pupil. The nun and the parents. The nun and the strap. The nun and the vegetables. The nun and the nun. The nun and the plane ticket. The nun and the university. The nun and the mother. The nun and Mother Ireland. Nun in a habit. Nun in a skirt and court shoes. Nun in a slacksuit. Nun on an expedition. Nun at a seminar. Nun in the suburbs. Nun in the city. Nun in the country. Nun in a taxi. Nun at the driver's side. Nun with glasses. Nun and kitten. Nun suffering the little children. Nun at the organ. Nun on a record cover. Nun with a bottle of brandy. Nun smoking a cigar. Nun on horseback. Nun on a tram. Nun in a pub. Smiling nun. Weeping nun. Melancholic nun. Jolly nun. Frozen nun. Sweaty nun. Nuns in the sea. Nuns around a bathing box. Nun in a sauna. Blushing nun. Bruised nun. Nun feeding the goldfish. Nun counting out the money. Nun throws herself off high-rise. Nun buries herself. Nun rises. Nun without a vocation. Nun on the road to heaven. Nun with an anklet of thorns. Nun with a diamond ring. Nun in the dark. Nun photographed. Nun without relatives. Freelance nun. Poor, chaste, obedient nun. And, finally, nun with a toothache.